Showdown

Red Rock Ranch ~ Book 2

BRITTNEY JOY

Brittney Joy/Brittney Joy Books
www.brittneyjoybooks.sqsp.com

Publisher's Note: This is a work of fiction. Names, characters, places, and incidents are a product of the author's imagination. Locales and public names are sometimes used for atmospheric purposes. Any resemblance to actual people, living or dead, or to businesses, companies, events, institutions, or locales is completely coincidental.

Showdown (Red Rock Ranch, book 2) / Brittney Joy: 1st ed.
ISBN-13: 978-1505332278
ISBN-10: 1505332273

"The horse is a great equalizer, he doesn't care how good looking you are, or how rich you are or how powerful you are-- he takes you for how you make him feel."

- Buck Brannaman

PROLOGUE

Taylor

THE SCREEN DOOR squeaked open and jolted me awake as it slapped shut. My heart pounded at the unwelcome sound, but I kept still, not wanting to open my eyes or move an inch off the cushioned lounge chair.

"You're going to be late for your lesson," Mom announced in her matter-of-fact tone, clicking across the deck. I peeked at her through squinted eyes, willing her heeled sandals and manicured toes to walk silently against the wood.

"Taylor, are you listening to me?" she continued, and I knew that my wish for silence wasn't going to happen.

I lifted my head, peeling my cheek from the

damp beach towel, rolling onto my back. "I'm not really in the mood for a lesson," I replied, using my arm to shield my face from the hot afternoon sun. I probably soaked up more sun than I should have, but I needed the time alone, away from the world. I was still fuming after losing the Cowboy Race this past weekend and everyone around this ranch reminded me of it. Especially Lucy.

"Don't be like that. Linda's staying at the ranch an extra week to help you prepare for that show this weekend," Mom said, smoothing out the front of her crisp, white linen pants and tucking her smooth blonde hair behind her ears. She wasn't looking at me while she was talking. "And, she's going to that thing with you tomorrow too."

I stared at her, wondering why she thought it was a good idea to wear white linen pants on a ranch. "And, by 'that thing,' are you referring to the awards ceremony for the Cowboy Race...*that I lost?*" I arched my eyebrows, waiting for her response.

She finally looked at me. "Don't be a sore loser, Taylor. And, don't be late for your lesson with Linda. Your father and I are paying good money for your trainer to stay here and work with you." And with that, Mom turned and headed down the stairs. Her heeled sandals clanked obnoxiously with each step. "I'm headed to the main cabin to have coffee with Mrs. Owens."

Sighing, I stood from the chair and let the towel drop to the floor. I adjusted the strings of my red bikini and leaned against the deck railing to watch her depart. My Mom didn't get it. Actually, she didn't get me. The "horse-stuff" was like a foreign language to her. No wonder she didn't understand why I was so pissed about losing the Cowboy Race.

I started riding when I was six years old. I've had countless lessons with a world class trainer and shown against serious competition. My horse's pedigree was filled with champions. And that dang Lucy girl shows up at the ranch and beats me on some crazy black horse she found wondering through the mountains?

I closed my eyes, my jaw clenched in frustration, but the darkness didn't ease my mind. With my eyes shut, images of the race flashed through my head and I dissected each move I should have done differently. I could have won. I *should* have won. The thought made my stomach turn.

Even though my Mom didn't know the first thing about horses, her last comment stuck in my head. I shouldn't be a sore loser. I knew I'd be sore for a while, but I definitely wasn't a loser. And, I needed to remind everyone of that.

ONE

Lucy

CHANCE STRETCHED INTO a long trot and I posted in the saddle. Moving along in a controlled bounce, I focused on keeping my heels down and my upper body still. I needed to stay balanced on his broad back, ready for anything - a spook, a jump. Chance and I were a new team and I was still learning his buttons.

"Sunny has to lope to keep up with Chance's trot!" Marilynn shouted with a giggle as the palomino mare reached Chance's side.

I smiled at the sight of Sunny. One of the dependable ranch horses, she was a sweet, bomb-proof mare that barely moved as she loped along. Marilynn, a fellow stablehand and new friend, looked like she was riding a golden rocking horse.

Chance seemed enchanted by Sunny as well, and cranked his head to get a better look at his riding partner. But, in doing so, he lost his balance and took an awkward stride sideways. I gathered the slack in my reins to correct his step, but wasn't quick enough. As we lurched to the side, my knee bumped into Sunny's shoulder.

"Oops, sorry," I said as I got Chance under control.

"No worries," Marilynn noted, patting the mare on her withers. "Nothing rattles this girl." She was right. I hoped Chance was learning a thing or two from Sunny.

As we approached the barn, the horses slowed to a walk and I scratched Chance's black neck. "What a good boy," I said, praising him for his efforts today. Chance lowered his head, relaxing into my touch. We still had a lot of work ahead of us, but Chance and I made leaps and bounds in a short time. We trusted each other now and that was half the battle.

"What else is on our to-do list for this afternoon?" I asked, referring to the list that Mr. Owens, the ranch owner and our boss, had written up this morning.

Marilynn brushed a loose strand of her brunette bob out of her face and pulled a piece of paper from her jean pocket, letting the reins rest on Sunny's neck. Sunny marched on like a little soldier as Marilynn read over the list.

"Let's see," she started. "What's left on the list for today? We moved the goats into the far pasture so they can eat down the blackberry bushes. We checked on the new heifers. Everyone is good there. Looks like all we have left to do is haul fresh salt blocks out to the pastures. We'll get the four-wheelers for that, though. Then we have a trail ride scheduled for this afternoon."

"Perfect," I noted, knowing how much I loved my summer job as a stablehand at the Red Rock Ranch. There wasn't a chore I didn't enjoy doing. Being around the horses all day, every day, was a dream. But, I did wonder when Mr. Owens would start giving me jobs with Casey again.

Ever since Mr. Owens stumbled upon a kiss Casey and I shared during the over-night camping trip, he had been keeping a close eye on us. Actually, Mr. Owens specifically stated that there would be nothing "inappropriate" going on under his watch and threatened to give my Dad a call if there was. I mean, it was just one kiss...*one kiss I relive over and over in my head every single night as I fall asleep.* Okay, maybe Mr. Owens did have a little something to worry about. Hopefully, he won't keep Casey and me apart all summer.

Throwing my leg over the saddle, I hopped

down from Chance. "Thanks for the ride, buddy," I said, rubbing my hands up and down his neck in a mini-massage. Chance leaned into his reward.

"If you take the horses back to the barn, I'll go get the four wheelers and start loading the salt blocks." Marilynn handed me the end of Sunny's reins. "Just put them both in the cross-ties. They can relax a bit before our trail ride."

I agreed, and gathered the leather reins. With one horse on each side of me, I started towards the barn.

Stepping through the open door and onto the concrete floor, my heart skipped a beat as my eyes scanned the building. On the opposite side of the aisle, the rusty farm truck was parked, the bed full of fresh hay bales. And, I realized what Casey's chore list consisted of today.

Reaching over the open tailgate, Casey grabbed a rectangular bale from the truck bed and hauled it off by its string twine. He effortlessly carried it to the corner of the barn, swung his torso, and launched the bale to the top of the pile. Pushing it tight against the stacked bales, Casey's defined arms were hard to ignore, especially since his t-shirt sleeves were pushed up, revealing his hard-earned muscles.

I sighed involuntarily and concentrated on walking so I wouldn't trip over my own feet.

Turning back towards the truck, Casey pushed

his sandy blonde hair from his eyes with a leather-gloved hand and noticed me watching him. He slowed for a second and shot me a smile - heat warmed my cheeks and I waved, the reins dangling from my hand. I tried to think of something clever or sweet to say, but words only jumbled around in my head without making a sentence.

The end of the Cowboy Race was a blur, but I specifically remember the hug Casey gave me after I dismounted. The crowd was cheering in the background and I had my head buried in Chance's black mane, both arms wrapped around his neck, tears of pure joy rolling down my face. Casey ran up behind me, spun me towards him and lifted me from the ground into a bear hug. If I hadn't been holding onto Chance's reins, I think he would have spun me in circles. It felt great...beyond amazing being wrapped in his arms and I wanted that feeling again. My heart pounded in my ears as I relived the scene, but the sharp beat of heels on cement broke my gaze.

Shiny black knee-high boots followed by clean tan breeches entered through the barn's center door and turned in my direction. Taylor. The heartbeat in my ears jumped straight to my chest.

The last time Taylor and I exchanged words was at the final jump of the Cowboy Race. She had been sitting in a puddle, drenched in mud, horseless, and defeated. But it wasn't her snarky comments that surprised me. It was the hint of gratitude in her eyes when she realized I had come back for her - to see if she was okay. I had never seen that side of Taylor before – the vulnerable side.

"Lucy," Taylor said in a minimal greeting as she strutted down the aisle and I realized I was standing directly in front of Star's stall.

"Hi Taylor," I responded, glancing side to side. Chance and Sunny were staring at me too, patiently waiting for me to lead them somewhere. Chance bumped my elbow with his nose, wondering what the holdup was. "Are you headed out on a ride? I'll get these guys out of your way."

"Lesson," she noted, pointing out my lack of specificity.

I took the hint. I clucked and the horses followed me as I got out of her way.

"Okay, do you need me to get you anything for your lesson?" I had to ask. No matter how rude Taylor was, she was still a paying guest at the ranch. And I worked here.

Taylor pushed Star's stall door open and the chestnut mare walked over to greet her. At least someone seemed happy to see her. She slipped a halter onto Star before responding, but never turned to face me.

"I don't need *your help*," she replied, and led Star out of her stall.

I forced myself to keep walking. I wanted to tell Taylor exactly what kind of help I thought she needed.

That was the Taylor I knew. I don't know what Taylor I got a glimpse of in that mud puddle.

Taylor

"I WANT HER stretching into the bit. Long and low," Linda announced from the middle of the sand arena. She adjusted the white visor on her head and followed me with her body as I trotted Star around the arena.

"Long and low and *forward*!" Linda shouted the last word and tossed her thick blonde braid over her shoulder so it fell down her back. "*Forward*, Taylor. You need to loosen her up. Prepare Star's muscles and ligaments for the workout."

At times Linda could be harsh, but she knew what she was doing. Years of lessons under her instruction had molded me into the rider I was today. She pushed me and critiqued me and eventually praised me – which was more than I could say of my own mother who barely paid attention to my rides. At the horse shows my Mom was more concerned with her social activity than my riding ability.

I squeezed Star's belly with a light touch of my

calves and felt her extend her trot underneath me. I lengthened my reins and Star lowered her neck, stretching her nose out to make contact with the bit. She was such a good girl. So smart and talented.

"Good, good. One more lap like that and then I want to see some serpentines," Linda said and then pointed to three evenly-spaced orange cones placed down the long center of the arena. "You are still warming her up so keep allowing her to reach out long and low with her neck. As you make your way through the serpentine, sit for one beat and then start posting with the opposite diagonal at each cone."

The exercise itself was not difficult for Star, or for me, and the rhythm of Star's smooth stride soothed me into a relaxed state.

"Good," Linda praised in a stern tone as I passed the last cone and continued trotting along the arena rail. "Now give me some shoulder rolls. Roll your shoulders back and loosen your own muscles. I want you both loose and ready. We are going to polish your lead changes today."

I loved lead changes. They were technical and magical. Being suspended in the air for a second between leads was a thrill. And, doing one right after the other felt like dancing.

Linda continued. "We'll get them polished up and nobody will be able to touch the two of you in your pattern classes at the show this weekend. Now, pickup your canter and start the serpentine again. At each cone I want to see a lead change."

A grin grew on my face – probably for the first time since the catastrophe of the Cowboy Race. So what if we got beat at some stupid race...it was practically a trail ride. It wasn't a real competition. Star was a show horse. I was a winner. And, I had a bedroom full of blue ribbons and golden trophies to prove it.

I gathered the reins in my hands and asked Star to move into a canter on the right lead. She rocked forward into her smooth stride without hesitation. Turning towards the first cone, I began to prepare for the lead change.

"Be conscious of your balance, Taylor," Linda reminded me. "Move with Star through the lead change. Don't throw her off."

In the last stride before we passed the cone, I straightened Star's body using my reins and my seat before moving my right leg back a few inches on her belly. Star collected her whole body and switched her lead effortlessly, cantering on. The following two lead changes were as smooth as the first. The graceful movements made me feel like a ballerina.

Linda applauded with three succinct claps. "Beautiful, beautiful. Now, canter on and try three lead changes on a straight line down the long side of the arena."

Star cantered on like a champ, her long flaxen mane rolling ever so slightly with each stride. Riding on, I patted her withers and mentally prepared myself for our next lead change. But, before we hit the long side of the arena, laughter broke my concentration and my gaze shot over my shoulder.

Marilynn and Lucy were leading a line of horses & giggling kids out for a trail ride. The group trotted along the dirt path next to the arena and Lucy waved as they passed by.

Star couldn't have cared less about the ruckus, but my jaw clenched at the sight of Lucy and that black horse. I looked away without responding and tried to focus on my riding.

As Star and I circled the end of the arena and started down the long side, I asked for the first lead change. Star picked her head up, but instead of changing her lead, she pinned her ears, kicked out, and then continued on with a few crow-hops.

"What the heck?" I yelled with a squeal before pulling Star to a stop. She still had her ears pinned as Linda walked towards us.

"What happened to your relaxation? Your focus?" Linda asked with a grimace on her face.

I knew exactly what happened to it, but I wasn't going to admit that some no-name girl had thrown off my game. "I don't know. I think Star is just being crabby or something."

Linda came to an abrupt stop next to Star's shoulder. "Look at your hands. Now. Look at them," she demanded and I followed orders.

Glancing down towards the saddle, I saw my hands locked in fists around the rich mahogany leather reins. My knuckles were actually white.

I immediately released the reins, letting them fall to Star's withers. She lowered her neck and I could have slapped myself. I just caused Star's tantrum.

Linda patted Star's copper chest. "Your mare is very sensitive. Very intuitive. Even when I first started her training as a two year old she responded to the slightest of touch. You have to be aware of your body and how you affect her."

I brushed my hand over Star's silky mane. "I'm sorry. That was my fault. It won't happen again."

"All right then. As long as you know you were the cause," Linda said as she turned to walk back to the center of the arena. "Again, please."

I gathered my reins and asked Star to walk off, knowing I still hadn't gotten over my loss to Lucy. I rolled my shoulders, loosening my back, and took a deep breath. I couldn't believe I let her get in my head.

TWO

Lucy

MR. OWEN'S MASSIVE Chevy truck rocked side to side as we pulled off the gravel road and inched onto the field. After a ten minute drive, we were now on the outskirts of Three Rivers - the small town closest to the ranch. I peeked over my shoulder and through the open window at the silver stock trailer, following the truck as we turned. Both Chance and Rocky peered through the slots on the side of the trailer, assessing the situation.

Chance let loose an ear piercing whinny. I closed my eyes and gripped the nylon seatbelt constricting my chest. I hated that he was stressed.

"He'll be fine. Don't worry your pretty little head," Marilynn reassured me and smiled from the front seat. "We're going to an awards ceremony, Lucy...an awards ceremony for a race you and Casey won. It's going to be fun."

I forced a polite smile. I appreciated Marilynn's encouragement, but my nerves were wound tight. Getting an award in front of the whole town of Three Rivers was not my idea of fun. I wanted to pick up the winning check and head back to the ranch. I wasn't sure why the town had to make such a big deal out of this.

Mr. Owens stopped the rig next to a line of shiny trailers and put it in park. People were milling around, brushing and saddling their horses.

"Ladies, we have arrived," he announced, grinning from ear to ear as he covered his gray hair with a black Stetson. I should have asked Mr. Owens if he wanted to accept the award on my behalf. He was reveling in the fact that his ranch was the talk of the town, on account of Casey and me.

I jumped out of the truck and climbed on the trailer fender to peek at the boys. Chance looked like a giraffe - his head cranked high in the air, surveying the scene outside the trailer. Next to my giraffe, Casey's horse was chewing on a mouthful of hay, unconcerned.

"Thanks for being so calm, Rocky," I whispered to the gray gelding through the open slot. "This is Chance's first time in a trailer. I'm glad he was with you." Actually, I was certain that Rocky was the only reason Chance arrived in one piece. "Hang-on, boys. We'll get you out of there in a few seconds."

I climbed down from the fender and hurried to the back of the trailer to find Casey and Dusty, one of the other ranch hands, a step ahead of me.

"Hey there," Casey greeted me with a smile as he swung open the back door of the trailer. "You ready for all this again?"

I nodded my head, but the look on my face must've given me away because Casey stepped closer and put a hand on my arm. "Chance will be fine, Lu. Once he knows you're here with him, he'll settle down." His blue eyes were full of certainty.

"Thanks," I replied. Casey's words managed to make me feel a bit better.

"Coming through," Dusty interrupted and Casey and I split apart, making room for him to lead Rocky out of the trailer. Stepping backwards, I brushed my fingers over my arm, grazing the very spot Casey had just held. I could still feel the heat from his touch.

Dusty moved Rocky to the side of the trailer and Casey stepped in. "Let me lead Chance out for you this time. I'm not exactly sure how he's going to unload." Casey's words were not a question, but he still looked to me for approval. "Is that okay?"

Chance's hooves beat against the floor as he

paced, shaking the trailer. I wanted to lead Chance out myself, but I nodded. I had to be reasonable - Casey had the strength to stop Chance from bursting out of the trailer. If I tried and couldn't stop him, we could both get injured. At my approval, Casey unlocked the steel divider. Chance whinnied at the top of his lungs, looking for Rocky.

"Easy boy," I said, faking a calm tone - and knowing I wasn't hiding my nerves from Chance.

Casey ran his hand up Chance's tense, sweaty neck and clipped the lead rope to his halter. Turning towards the open door, Chance began trotting in place, but Casey held tight to the lead. With his neck curled and nostrils flared, Chance looked like a live grenade - one that could go off at any second. I wanted them both out of that tiny rectangular space as soon as possible.

Reaching the edge of the trailer, Casey stepped down, but Chance bulked, snorting at the new smells ahead of him. Casey moved to the side, leaving slack in the lead rope and allowing Chance time to relax...but Chance decided he wanted out.

Picking up his front legs, Chance held himself in a half-rear like a Lippizzaner Stallion in a Levade. I sucked in my breath, imagining his head hitting the trailer ceiling and trampling Casey on his way out.

Instead, Chance launched himself out of the trailer in one smooth motion, landing squarely in front of Casey and me.

I let out my breath and Casey chuckled. Chance looked like he surprised himself as well.

"Disaster averted," Casey said. "Looks like we need to practice that maneuver back at the ranch."

"I'll put 'trailer unloading' on the to-do list," I noted with a straight face as Casey handed me the lead line. I made sure I had a good grip.

Taylor

Star's silky mane slid through my fingers as I finished one long braid which accented her slender neck. The pink ribbon laced through her flaxen hair was the perfect touch. Satisfied with my work, I patted the end of the braid and grabbed the bottle of ShowSheen from the horse trailer tack room.

"You're a show pony," I whispered to Star as I sprayed the ShowSheen on a towel and wiped the polish down her neck, chest, and finally over her crisp white blaze. "These ranch horses got nothing on you."

I reached into my pocket and Star's ears perked forward at the crinkling of a peppermint. I smiled as she lapped the treat out of my hand in one swift motion and then nuzzled my pockets, looking for more.

"Better get her bridled," Linda said as she threw the reins over Cash's withers and stepped into the saddle. Linda's heavily muscled buckskin had an appropriate name. Cash was a world champion barrel racer and I'd watched Linda rake in the titles from his back. Cash wasn't used to settling for second place either.

"Okay, let's get this over with," I muttered and offered Star one more peppermint before grabbing her bridle from the trailer.

The entire town of Three Rivers crowed the sidewalks of Main Street. Little kids lined the curbs, ogling the horses and snatching up candies. The mayor and his family led the front of the parade - siting in an antique truck waving at the crowd as they rolled down the pavement.

Star and Cash walked side by side, their metal shoes clinking against the asphalt as we followed the trivial procession. Even though it was painful, I forced myself into rodeo-queen mode. Sitting up stick-straight and pushing my shoulders back, I cupped my hand and began a slow wave.

"I *hate* that we have to ride behind Lucy and Casey," I griped to Linda between gritted teeth while keeping a smile plastered on my face.

"Well, Ms. Taylor. They won," Linda said matter-of-factly as she scanned the spectators. "They were better than us. Take note and let's not allow that to happen again."

Linda's words hit me like a slap across the face and I lost my smile as they sank in. Not only did I let myself down, I had disappointed Linda.

My hand continued in a slow waving motion, but my eyes narrowed in on the two riders ahead of me. That crazy black horse pranced next to Rocky like a Thoroughbred being ponied to the starting gate. And, when Chance jigged sideways and bounced off of Rocky, Casey reached out for Lucy's shoulder.

I cringed as Casey slid his fingers down Lucy's arm and grabbed hold of her hand, squeezing it tight. But, something clicked as I watched Lucy relax with his touch...and then Chance slowed to a walk.

Casey was Lucy's confidence. He was the glue that kept Lucy from falling apart under pressure. She couldn't have won that race without him. She couldn't have beaten me without him.

Now, it's time I break her glue.

THREE

Lucy

DRAPED ACROSS MY chest, the pearl white sash fluttered in the wind as I hopped down from the wooden stage. My feet hit the grass and I was thankful the ceremony was coming to an end. The chaos was over and the most important thing was tucked safely in my pocket - the prize money. Running my hand over the bulge in my jean pocket, I reassured myself that Chance would *officially* be my horse after today.

I straightened my sash and turned to Casey. "I'm surprised they didn't give us crowns."

Casey chuckled. "Enjoy the spotlight for a bit, Lucy. We earned it. Besides, I think you'd look pretty good in a tiara." He winked at me and my heart palpitated as he reached out his hand. "Would my winning race partner care to join me for a dance...to celebrate?"

With my heart thumping, I froze up. I didn't dance. I was born with two left feet and they only worked together in the saddle. "Um, I'm not sure you want me stepping on your feet."

"Come on," Casey urged and grabbed my hand. His touch pulsed electricity through my fingers. "I'm not taking 'no' for an answer. I wore my steel-toe boots. You can stand on my feet for all I care."

Not waiting for a response, Casey turned to pull me away from the stage and onto the field, now filled with country music and dancing couples. He didn't have to pull hard. I followed.

Casey weaved his way into the center of the bouncing crowd and turned back to me. He raised my hand – the one he was holding - and gently placed his opposite arm against the middle of my back. My free hand fell naturally on his shoulder, against the crisp cotton of his button-down shirt.

I looked straight into his baby blue eyes and swallowed hard, hoping he couldn't feel me tremble. "I hope you're good at leading," I warned, and wondered if I'd be this nervous dancing with anyone else.

Casey grinned and his dimples appeared. "Don't you worry, Ms. Lucy. I won't throw out any of my fancy dance moves...not just yet."

Casey's dimples didn't make me any less nervous, but I couldn't keep myself from smiling. Feeling my cheeks flush, I looked away, hoping my face wasn't fire-engine red. I had to focus on my feet and looking at Casey's handsome face was too much of a distraction.

We started with little steps, rocking in a small circle. Casey kept enough tension in his arms to firmly direct my body and soon we were keeping beat with the band.

Gazing over Casey's shoulder and past the crowd, a glimpse of the open field reminded me why we were here. "Can you believe we were riding Chance and Rocky across this grass just a few days ago? Galloping them across the finish line?"

"I can believe it," Casey said with confidence as he lifted my hand to turn me in a spin. "We make quite the team."

I'm not sure if it was the directional change or Casey's statement, but my mind lost track of where my feet were going. Instead of completing a ladylike spin, I tripped myself with my own foot. The tip of my boot caught on my opposite ankle and attempts to yank it loose only pushed me further off balance. I knew I was going to fall (not so gracefully) to the dance floor and I couldn't even force out a whimper in protest of my clumsiness.

But, to my surprise, Casey managed to keep hold of my hand as I spun. Still gripping tight to my fingers, Casey's arm wrapped around my waist and his opposite arm grabbed my back – keeping me from suffering a face-plant to the grass.

Now cradled in his arms, I stared at Casey's hypnotizing eyes and perfect white smile – lingering only a few inches from my lips. "I told you." I shrugged my shoulders sheepishly. "Two left feet."

Casey laughed, his sandy blonde hair grazing his eyes. "Well, that's one way to get close to you."

The few inches between us held a clear tension. If I had known this position would come from my clumsiness, I would've been tripping all over the ranch.

Then the music stopped...or at least I think it stopped. I couldn't really tell because I was stuck in my own world – with Casey. And, the rest of the universe fell away as he held me.

"Attention race participants." The speakers crackled. "Attention race participants. In ten minutes we will be taking a group picture in the field. Please saddle your horses and bring your trophies."

The heat rushed back to my cheeks as I pulled my feet underneath myself to stand upright. I knew Casey caught me blush that time.

Letting go of me, Casey cleared his throat. "I guess I'll go get our trophies from the stage." His statement lacked his earlier confidence. "Meet you back at the trailer to saddle up the horses?"

"Yeah. Sure. Sounds good." The words fell out of my mouth faster than I could think them. I wished that had happened anywhere but here - in the middle of all these people, with Mr. Owens looming in the background.

I wanted Casey to kiss me. I wanted to kiss him. A lot. A lot more than I wanted to go get my picture taken.

"I'll see you in a few minutes then," Casey said without breaking his gaze.

"Yeah, in a few minutes," I replied and forced myself to turn away. I started walking before a full on kiss-fest was broadcast to the whole town of Three Rivers...and we both put ourselves in danger of losing our jobs.

Walk it off, Lucy. Walk it off.

My mind was cluttered with images of Casey as I approached the horse trailer - his perfect smile, his bronze skin, his broad shoulders. I had never been so fixated with someone before. What was wrong with me? I shook my head back and forth, trying to jar the images from my mind.

Luckily, Chance's familiar low nicker brought

me back to reality, reminding me that the horses needed to be saddled. I looked ahead to see Chance's ebony coat and Rocky's gray dapples shining in the sunshine. The two geldings were tied to the stock trailer, happily eating from their hay nets.

"Hey there, buddy," I sighed and rolled my hand down the length of his forehead, wondering what I was going to say to Casey when he got here with the trophies. We'd already been warned. It was clear we weren't to be getting too close. Kissing was definitely out of the question. I needed to rein in these feelings before I got myself in trouble.

Chance watched me with his soft brown eyes as he grabbed another mouthful of hay. He seemed to be analyzing my thoughts as he chewed.

"Don't judge me, Chance." I grinned. "I don't know where these feelings came from...or what to do with them. Any advice for me?"

I scratched along his neck with my fingertips, thinking I should get the saddles out of the trailer just as Chance stopped chewing. He raised his head, his ears forward and alert.

I stopped scratching. "Did you spot Casey?" I whispered, wishing Chance could actually give me a piece of advice. I took another deep breath before turning around. I had to play it cool. *Play it cool, Lucy. Play it cool.*

I spun on my heels and started blabbing before I

could get lost in Casey's eyes. "I guess we better get these guys tacked up for the --" But my words stopped midsentence as I locked in on the man standing before me.

"Mr. Jackson," I exhaled abruptly. Billy Jackson - Chance's former owner. Or, Chance's *soon-to-be* former owner. I still had to give Billy the prize money from the race. And, he still had to sign over Chance's registration papers to me.

"I prefer Billy," he replied and stepped forward. In the tiny space between the trailers, I immediately realized we were isolated from the crowd. And Billy's presence gave me the creeps. The last time I was alone with him I got pushed to the ground and bounced off a fence board. I wanted to get this transaction done as quickly as possible.

I grabbed the check from my back pocket and handed it to him. "Here it is. Here's the check for $5,000. I had the race committee make it out in your name."

I expected Billy to snatch it from my hand and throw Chance's registration papers at me. Instead, he cocked his head and spit a line of brown tobacco juice from the side of his mouth. A grin grew on his face, revealing his yellowed teeth.

The check dangled between us.

"Here," I said again. The small piece of paper was starting to feel heavy between my fingers.

"I don't want the $5,000 anymore," he announced without blinking.

I was certain I didn't hear him right.

"What?" The word creaked out of my mouth and my heart began thumping against my rib cage. "What do you mean?"

Billy adjusted the bill of his dusty ball cap and raised his chin. "He's a race winner, right? Seems like he should be worth more than $5,000."

Billy stood, unwavering, in front of me and I couldn't wrap my head around his statement. Did this low-life just ask me for more money?...because *Chance and I* won the Cowboy Race?

"You want more money for Chance?" The words fell from my mouth, followed by my heart, as his intentions fully hit me. I glanced back at Chance, not wanting to take my eyes off Billy for long. Chance was pacing. I wanted to console him, to tell him not to worry, but I didn't know what Billy was planning to do.

I tried to slow my breathing, not wanting this monster of a man to know I was scared – terrified that he would take Chance from me. "You said $5,000. You can't go back on your word...you just can't." I couldn't believe this was happening. He didn't even want Chance. The only thing he cared about was squeezing every dollar he could get out of "his" horse. "Five thousand dollars was the deal!" I caught myself in a scream as I turned away, reaching for Chance's lead. I pulled at the end of the rope, releasing the knot and freeing Chance from the trailer. There was no way this creep was taking my horse.

Billy was now walking towards us and I knew I had to get out of there, fast. "Give me the horse," he grumbled, reaching out his hand.

"No! Get away!" The words shot out of my throat and I threw the lead over Chance's withers. I braced myself to jump on his back and gallop far, far away when a female voice jumped in.

"What the heck is going on?" Taylor asked as she appeared from under the front gooseneck of the horse trailer. She held a bridle in one hand and a second place trophy in the other. "It sounds like a freaking Jerry Springer show over here."

Taylor was not who I wanted to see, but at least I had a witness so this lunatic wouldn't assault me again. "He's going to take Chance," I sputtered out and pointed at Billy. Tears were gravitating to my eyes.

Taylor crossed her arms and threw her blonde braid behind her shoulders with one flick of her head. "Oh for God's sake, Lucy. Are you sure?"

By this time, Linda had wondered over and was also checking out the scene. I looked from Taylor to Billy and back again. "Yes, Taylor," I shouted, baffled at her question. I didn't have time for her backhanded comments. "Yes, I'm sure. He just asked me for more money and I don't have any more to give."

Taylor's forehead wrinkled up in confusion. "I thought that horse was already yours."

"He should be," I said, swallowing my tears and wanting to spit them at Billy.

Taylor paused and the confusion left her face. She shifted her eyes away from me, to Billy. "How much do you want for him?" Her question came out in an even, cool tone.

"Ten Grand." Billy threw out the number without a moment's hesitation, focusing his sights on Taylor.

"What?!" Billy wanted $10,000, double the money I had, and now Taylor was offering to buy Chance? Every protective instinct I had was gnawing at my gut, telling me to stop the insanity. "You can't have him! Either of you!" The ground felt like it was spinning and I held tight to a chunk of Chance's thick mane, balled in my fist.

"Settle down, Lucy. Crazy doesn't look good on you," Taylor said and looked at me with one eyebrow cocked while executing a half-roll with her eyes. "I don't want him."

Was this some kind of sick game?

Taylor nodded her head towards Linda. "Can

you grab my checkbook from the trailer? It's in my purse in the living quarters."

Linda froze for a second, probably just as confused as I was. "Are you buying half of that black horse? Don't you want to run that by your parents first?"

Linda's questions seemed valid, but Taylor looked annoyed by them. "I'll just buy a few less pairs of boots this month and tell my Mom I needed a new show outfit. They'll never even miss the money," she answered. "And, no, I'm not buying half of that horse."

Taylor's eyes never left mine through her explanation. She was talking directly to me. "I'll give Billy the additional $5,000 if you agree to work for me for one weekend." She paused before continuing, probably soaking in the shock on my face. "Linda's assistant broke her arm on a spill off a colt yesterday so she can't work at my show this weekend. We need someone to feed, pick stalls, groom, clean tack...someone to do all the chores no one else wants to do."

Linda stared at Taylor with her mouth gaped open but snapped it shut when she realized she was announcing her shock to everyone.

Billy spat another line of tobacco juice from his mouth. "I don't care where the money comes from. Get it to me and that horse is yours. Otherwise, I'm taking him with me right now. I'm sure I can get $10,000 out of someone else."

My pulse flicked violently against the side of my neck. I knew Taylor was basically asking me to be her slave for the weekend. I had no idea what I was in for or why she would even offer up the money, but I knew I could make it through one weekend of anything in order to keep Chance – to make him mine. I locked eyes with Taylor and shook my head up and down. I was in.

I laid flat on top of my quilt, staring at the A-frame wooden ceiling of my bunk. Today had sucked every ounce of energy from my body. I considered falling asleep in my clothes, but the thought of laying in filth all night gave me motivation to move towards the shower - a little motivation anyhow.

My fingers rubbed tiny circles on the thick paper pressed to my chest, reassuring myself that it was real. I raised the paper to eye level and examined the text I had already read a million times during the truck ride back to the ranch.

Chance's registered name was "Fool's Gold" and he was seven years old, registered to the American Quarter Horse Association. The picture in the corner of his papers showed a spindly, long legged foal standing close to the golden rump of his mother. His brown fuzzy coat and curly mohawk were a far cry from the stark black, strong gelding I knew today. But, his trusting brown eyes were the same. The picture made me smile.

But, what really made me smile was the back of the paper. The back of the paper was solely text and I scanned over my favorite part – the signature of the seller, Billy Jackson, and the signature of the new owner, Lucy Rose. Chance and I officially belonged to one another. This paper told me so.

I hugged the paper to my chest again and felt myself drifting to sleep. My eyelids slipped shut and I decided it wasn't so bad to sleep in dirty jeans.

FOUR

Taylor

I SAT ON top of my teal blue suitcase, yanking the zipper shut and examining my pile of luggage. I had one massive suitcase, a matching teal tote bag, a boot bag, a cowboy hat case, and a purse – all of which needed to be hauled across the ranch and loaded into my horse trailer. How was I supposed to do that by myself? If I was at home, one of the maids would have already taken care of it. Annoyed, I stood up and reluctantly gathered my essentials for the weekend.

The wheels on my suitcase rolled smoothly across the wooden floors of the cabin, but maneuvering around furniture with the stack of bags was quite the task. Heading through the living room, my boot bag caught on a floor lamp, knocking it to the ground in a crash. I jumped forward, startled, and managed to trip over a pair of particularly high heeled gold sandals which sent me stumbling out the screen door, my suitcase nipping at my heels.

Catching my balance outside the door, I growled to myself. Only my Mom would pack a pair of gold stilettos for our summer trip to the ranch. I cursed the gold sandals as I gathered my bags – which were now scattered across the deck.

"You okay, Taylor?" A concerned voice asked from the walking path below the deck.

Peeking over the railing, I recognized the boy in khaki cargo shorts and a Broncos baseball hat. Andy from Denver. Yesterday he wandered over, uninvited, while I was sunbathing – in my bikini. He was here with his uncle or something. Just got here a few days ago and was staying in the cabin a few doors down.

Andy was no cowboy, but I was sure those broad shoulders could carry a suitcase. Otherwise it was going to be a long walk to the horse trailer.

I gave my suitcase a push with my knee and waited for it to topple over, banging against the wooden boards. "Oh my goodness," I exclaimed and gave a loud sigh. I tossed my hair over my shoulder like a pro and walked across the deck to lean on the railing. "Hey, Andy. What you up to?" I marveled at my soap-opera dramatics.

"Do you need some help?" he asked.

"Oh, that would be great. Do you mind? I just need to get these bags to my horse trailer. They're so heavy." I cocked my head and raised my eyebrows. "I don't want to bother you if you're busy, though."

I watched Andy's well-muscled calves flex as he flew up the stairs to the deck. Mr. Athlete grabbed all of my bags before I moved an inch off the railing. "No problem. Glad to help," he said and flashed a smile.

I wrinkled my nose and gave Andy my signature grin. "Well, aren't you just a sweetheart."

Boys - they all fall for the same thing.

On the trek to the trailer, I complimented Andy on his gentleman-like behavior. "Oh, Andy. You've been such a big help." I unlocked and opened the door to the trailer's living quarters and stepped aside. It was amazing what a little ego-stroking could get you.

"No problem," he said as he tossed my bags in and handed me my purse. "Maybe we can hangout when you get back from your horse show? I'll be here all week."

"I'm sure we can." I winked at his trusting face,

knowing we wouldn't hangout when I got back.

"Are you ready to load the horses?" Lucy's overly sweet voice rang through the air and I peered around Andy.

Lucy stood at the back of the horse trailer with a small duffel bag slung over her shoulder. Her mousy brown hair was slapped into a slick ponytail, like always, and there wasn't a stitch of makeup on her face. And, Casey was standing at her side. I didn't understand what he saw in her.

"Yeah, Linda will be here in a few minutes," I said, the annoyance in my voice audible. "I'll get Star and then you can load Chance." I turned my attention back to Andy. His clean-cut, city-slicker look was no match for Casey's worn Wranglers and farm-earned muscles. "Have a good weekend." I patted Andy on the shoulder and walked towards the barn without looking back. I was done flirting.

Lucy

I sat in the backseat of the truck wishing I didn't get motion sickness from reading. The horse magazines I packed were peeking out the top of my bag, taunting me, but I figured I better wait to read them. About the only thing that could increase the tension in this cab would be to puke all over the soft leather seats.

The hour long drive to the show grounds contained only essential conversation. There was no chit-chat from Linda as she drove or from Taylor in the passenger seat. In fact, in the first few minutes of the ride, Taylor turned the radio to a country station and glued her eyes to her phone's screen.

I was thankful the scenery out the window kept me entertained during our silent trip. The highway to Bend, Oregon was lined with rustic ranches and fields full of livestock. I watched two young girls canter their horses through a lazy herd of cattle...and the scene brought my thoughts back to Chance.

Yesterday, when Taylor said I could bring Chance with to the show, I was relieved. He gave me a sense of comfort and I knew I needed his presence to help me through the weekend. Plus, it would be good for him to experience new things. We could experience them together.

I'd never been to a horse show of this caliber. In the little information Taylor gave me, she explained that we were headed to the Northwest Stock Horse Championships. Since then, I'd been imagining insanely expensive horses stalled up in pristine barns and accomplished riders walking the show grounds. This was going to be a foreign world for Chance and for me.

And, to prove my imagination right, Linda

slowed the rig as we approached what seemed like miles of bright white fencing. I gasped as the truck turned down the long paved driveway that ran between the manicured fields. The green pasture on our right housed a small herd of broodmares with babies at their sides. They grazed happily as their coats gleamed in the sun. And, the pasture on our left enclosed a group of spunky yearlings frolicking through the grass.

Peeling my eyes away from the prancing babies, I looked ahead to find the biggest barn I had ever seen. The sprawling building was covered in cream siding with green trim and a matching roof. The highest part of the barn was lined with classic square cupolas, topped with horse-shaped weather vanes. The gorgeous barn looked like it had been ripped from the pages of *Horse Illustrated*.

Coasting along, we followed a line of trucks and trailers as the driveway morphed into a circle - surrounding a colorful rose bed and a massive bronze horse. The metal statue seemed to watch our rig as we circled it and parked in the unloading area. Yep, I was out of my league.

Linda put the truck in park and grabbed her purse from the seat. "All right, girls. I'm headed to the show office to get us signed in. You two can unload the horses. Taylor, you know where our stalls are."

All three of us hopped out of the truck and into the chaos of the unloading area. Metal shoes clip-clopped along the pavement as horses stepped off trailers and were guided to the barn. Horses whinnied greetings to each other as their people pushed wheelbarrows full of feed and polished tack. People and horses marched in every direction, but it was controlled chaos. Everyone seemed to know where they were going. Except me.

Following Taylor to the back of the trailer, I waited for more instructions. She unlatched and opened the double doors. "Unload Chance and wait for me. You can follow me to the stalls."

"Okay," I replied as she handed me a lead rope.

I stepped into the trailer and unclipped the metal separator which kept Chance standing in one place during the ride. Swinging open the metal half-wall, I watched Chance curl his neck towards me, the whites of his eyes showing. His neck and chest were damp with sweat, but he was in one piece...unharmed. And, it didn't look like he did any damage to Taylor's trailer. Thank God.

"Don't worry, Chance," I reassured him as I clipped the lead rope to his halter and lead him towards the rear of the trailer. "We are just here for the weekend. It'll be fun. It's good to try new things."

As we edged towards the back of the trailer, I

gripped the lead rope in preparation for Chance's projectile launch to the pavement. I squeezed tight, hoping I could hold on.

Chance hesitated at the floor's edge, but actually followed me to the ground with just a hop. I breathed a sigh of relief and turned to pat him on the neck. "See. We're getting better at this stuff."

Chance didn't notice my pat. His ears were pricked forward, but he was *not* paying attention to me. His eyes darted around, evaluating the busy parking lot, and his head inched higher and higher with each passing second. I felt like I was holding onto a kite in a wind storm.

"Follow me," Taylor instructed as she unloaded Star from the trailer and turned towards the barn.

I followed, hoping Chance would relax in Star's presence, but he seemed to think his friend was running away from him. Chance danced at the end of the lead rope and put his whole body into a whinny that made my ears ring. His sides quivered from the force of his shriek.

Taylor shot an annoyed look over her shoulder and my grip on Chance's lead rope couldn't get any tighter. "Easy, buddy. Star isn't leaving us. We're going with her." I hoped the stalls weren't far away. Chance needed some time to chill out in this new environment – in a safely enclosed space.

Taylor walked Star through the open barn door

and into one of the aisles, which wasn't any quieter than the unloading area. Star sashayed down the center of the aisle with slack in her lead rope as Taylor nodded and waved to acquaintances. They smiled back as Taylor passed, but their facial expressions changed as soon as they laid eyes on me. And, they moved out of my way - fast.

Chance's hind end swayed side to side in protest of my slow speed and I was certain we were going to plow through anything in our way. He pulled me along like a water-skier while still prancing on his tip-toes.

I wanted to turn him in a circle, to break his focus and calm him down, but there was no room to do it. Expensive saddles, tack boxes, brooms, and wheelbarrows cluttered the aisle.

"Chance, come on," I whispered through gritted teeth and gave him a quick yank on the lead rope. He didn't acknowledge my tug and I wasn't sure how long I could hold him back. Panic sank in as I realized I was losing a battle with a thousand pound horse.

Just then, Taylor turned Star into a stall. Looking at me through the metal bars, she nodded her head towards the next stall. "You can put Chance in there."

Without stopping or saying a word, I aimed Chance towards the open door and leapt through. He nearly stomped my toes as he followed, trotting into the cedar bedding with a snort.

I slammed the door shut behind us.

We made it.

Thankful he was now enclosed, I peeled off Chance's halter and snuck out of the stall to watch him pace from a safe distance. He circled the square space and screamed into the air, nostrils flared. Star responded by pinning her ears flat to her neck and flipping her head towards Chance, apparently telling Chance to shut his mouth.

"Well, this should be interesting," Taylor said, coming up beside me and crossing her arms.

Her statement crept into my head and I suddenly wondered if it was a bad idea to bring Chance along.

FIVE

Taylor

I RAN MY fingers over the embroidery on the back of the tall director's chair. The horse image circled by gold lettering looked sharp against the black fabric, but it was the words that brought a smile to my face – "California Stock Horse Grand Champion" followed by my name, Taylor Johnson.

I took a sip of my iced latte, reading the words a few more times before I hopped into the seat. I crossed my legs and spread a glossy magazine over my lap. But before I flipped through the pages, I lingered on the cover – a picture of last year's Northwest Stock Horse Champion. The girl's face beamed with pride from atop her horse while surrounded by family, friends, and trainers. And next to the winner sat a massive gold trophy and an engraved saddle.

I wanted that. I wanted that trophy, that saddle, that picture, that moment. And, I knew Star and I could do it. We could take the championship title this weekend...and next year our picture would be featured on the cover. The thought made my stomach flutter in anticipation.

Breaking into my daydream, Star reached her neck over the fabric guard on the stall door. She nuzzled my shoulder, sniffing for a treat.

"You want it too, don't you?" I whispered before pulling a peppermint from my pocket. Star's brown eyes widened at the crinkle of the wrapper and she gobbled the candy from the palm of my hand. I gave her a kiss on her smooth muzzle. "You sure would look pretty in that championship saddle."

Star blew a few soft breaths against my cheek before she pinned her ears and bit at the stall bars, forcing Chance to step back. I chuckled at her mare-ish behavior. "I know, I know. He's annoying. But, at least he stopped screaming at the top of his lungs." Star popped her ears forward and focused her attention back on me. Sniffing around for another treat, she got a whiff of my latte and nuzzled the plastic cup while I took a drink.

"When is your first class tomorrow, Ms. Taylor?" The cheery voice caught me off guard and I looked up from my drink, mid-sip.

"Hey, Tim. I was wondering where you were. When did you get in?" Tim Green, Linda's husband, came to every show. He didn't ride, but he was there supporting Linda and her clients. He hauled horses, kept them fed, and was our biggest cheerleader.

Tim set down an armful of fabric - the stall decor - and brushed off his polo shirt before walking over to give me a hug. "Left California late last night and got here a few hours ago with the trailer and horses." He put his hands on his hips and took a breath. "So how are my favorite princesses doing?"

Tim called everyone sweetheart or darling or dear. He referred to Linda as *baby*, but Star and I were his only princesses. His nickname always made me feel special.

"We're good." I smiled. "And, our first class is western horsemanship tomorrow. Probably about 9:00 or so."

"I'll be there with bells on," Tim replied as he grabbed a footstool and carried it across the aisle.

Lucy made her way from the back of the barn and joined him, another stall drape under her arm.

"Lucy, can you grab the bucket of clasps over there? I'll need you to hand them to me as I hang these up." Lucy did as she was told and stood next to the footstool, handing Tim clasps as he hung the hunter green drapery from the top of the horse stalls.

"I could get used to having you around, Lucy. I'm usually doing this all by myself while the girls ride." Tim chuckled. "It's quite the scene."

"Glad to help, Tim. That's what I'm here for."

Could she be any more of a suck-up? I closed my magazine and hopped off my chair. "Speaking of riding - I'm going to saddle up and practice my pattern for tomorrow morning. Star needs to stretch her legs."

"All right. Linda will be looking for you soon anyhow. She's outside by the practice pens," Tim noted, as he set the last clasp in place and stepped down from the footstool to admire his work. "Sure does look classy when it's all set up. Doesn't it, girls?"

"Looks great, Tim," I said. Tim always did a wonderful job of setting up our show barn. All of our stalls were now covered in hunter green drapery sporting Linda Green's name in bold, gold lettering. The aisle was lined with potted plants, sporting red and white flowers, and a cute table and chair set completed the vision.

Scanning the setup, I was reminded of the two empty stalls across the aisle. I wondered which horses Tim hauled in for the show. Whoever they were, I was ready to go find them.

<>&<>&<>

Lucy

I tucked the nearly empty bucket of metal clasps back inside the tack trunk and closed the heavy lid. Completing a full turn, I couldn't believe I was standing in a horse stall. It was unrecognizable after Tim and I unloaded Taylor and Linda's trailers, filling the space with tack, show clothes, brushes and feed.

The walls were covered with a thick, hanging fabric which matched the hunter green drapery on the front of the stalls and the floor was padded with a checkerboard of rubber mats. A small radio in the corner played soft country music and I closed my eyes to inhale the scent of clean leather. The tack room was like my own little world, quiet and drama-free.

I could hear Chance in the next stall, finally munching on his hay, and I pictured myself curled up in a folding chair reading a book. That sounded like heaven.

But, I knew I had a full list of chores to complete today. No reading just yet. Instead, I pulled the draped door aside and stepped out of the tack room. In the aisle, Taylor had Star cross-tied and was fiddling with her saddle. I was glad she was heading out for a ride. She hadn't said much to me today, but she made up for the lack of communication in the form of evil stares.

I still didn't understand why she wanted me at her show – except that Linda was down an assistant. I guess the thought of doing any real work was enough to make Taylor put up with me. I knew the only reason I was putting up with her was because she wrote me a check, and helped me keep Chance.

"What's next on the list, Tim?"

He wiped his brow with the back of his hand and pondered my question. "Well, my stomach is starting to growl. I think I'm going to round up some lunch for us all. How do sub sandwiches sound, girls?"

"Sounds good," Taylor and I said in unison, catching each other's gaze and breaking it just as quickly.

"Okay, lunch will be served for the Green Team in about an hour." Tim grabbed his ring of keys from the table and chair set. "Taylor, can you let the rest of the gang know?"

"Will do," she said, while buckling the throat latch on Star's bridle.

"Actually Taylor, why don't you take Lucy with you to the practice pen? Show her around the grounds a bit while I go get lunch."

Taylor was gathering the reins in her hands, but stopped abruptly at Tim's suggestion. I was expecting a sharp comment to follow, but she gave us a stiff smile instead.

"Sure," Taylor noted and turned to me with the slight raise of an eyebrow.

"You girls have fun. I'll see you in a bit." He waved as he exited the aisle. Tim didn't realize he was sending me off with the enemy.

I followed Taylor, but kept my distance, as she led Star through the barn and into the unloading area, now occupied by just a few straggler trailers. The chaos of unpacking had dwindled and I wondered if everyone was out to lunch.

Walking along the barn, still in silence, we passed the wide entrance to the indoor arena. The metal lights blared bright from the ceiling and a single tractor spun circles in the sand footing, making it smooth. There wasn't a single soul riding around the rail.

"The main arena is closed to riders until the show starts tomorrow morning," Taylor noted. "And the warm-up arenas are located on the side of the barn. That's where we're going."

We turned around the corner of the barn and I could see where everyone was. There were three large outdoor arenas – the practice pens. They sat side-by-side and were packed with horses. Horses and riders moved in every direction – left, right, circles, straight. It was basically a three-ring circus.

"The middle arena is for pleasure horses. That's where I'm going to ride Star," Taylor said, putting a boot in the stirrup and grabbing hold of the reins.

"Do you want me to hold Star while you get on?" I offered, feeling like I wasn't doing much just standing there and watching.

"No, she's fine," Taylor responded before hopping into the saddle with the grace of a gymnast. "I see Linda. Follow me. I'm sure she has more stuff for you to do."

I followed - a little concerned that I was going to be run over on our way to the practice pens. Horse traffic was everywhere. *They should have a pedestrian crossing out here or something.*

Nearing the arenas, I spotted Linda too, standing next to the white fence and completely focused on the riders ahead of her.

"Ask him to jog. Relax. You're doing fine out there," Linda said with her arms crossed, not acknowledging our presence as we walked up beside her. "Make sure to keep your heels down and your elbows at your sides."

Taylor sat straight-backed and quiet in the saddle but she must've caught the look of confusion on my face.

"Linda's talking to one of her clients in the

ring," Taylor noted and then pointed to her ear. "She has a headset on."

Oh. That made a little more sense. I was starting to wonder if Linda had lost her marbles and was muttering riding instructions to herself.

"Where's her client?" I asked, glad to have *something* to talk to Taylor about. I scanned the masses of riders making their way around the ring and noticed many of them were wearing headsets or Bluetooth devices. A line of trainers stood outside the arena, directing from the sidelines.

Taylor was scanning the crowd, too. "I'm not sure which of Linda's clients came here for the show."

"Tiera," Linda said, still not facing us, and then continued with her instructions. "That's it. Keep him jogging. That's a good pace."

"Oh. Great," Taylor grumbled and locked her eyes on someone in the crowd. I couldn't tell if her comment was meant to be sarcastic or if she was just being herself. Sarcasm seemed to be Taylor's form of communication.

She sighed and pointed to the opposite side of the pen. "See the gray horse with the baby pink saddle pad? That's Georgie and the rider is Tiera."

I stretched onto my tippy-toes and bobbed back and forth until I could get a good look through the commotion of the ring. But once I did, Tiera was hard to miss.

"Yeah, I see her."

Tiera's horse was pale gray, nearing white, and his pink gear popped against his light-colored coat. In fact, she had her horse decked out in pink – pink saddle pad, pink split boots, and pink crystals on her bridle and breast-collar. Not to mention, Ms. Tiera was sporting pink cowboy boots and a matching blouse. The color complemented her tanned skin and white blonde hair which was wrapped in a tight bun at the nape of her neck. Her horse jogged around at a perfect tempo, with a perfect headset. He didn't blink an eye at the horses bobbing and weaving around him.

I exhaled in defeat. Tiera - even her name screamed 'princess'. I was going to have to put up with two divas this weekend. Lord, help me.

"That's good, Tiera. Walk him now and cool him down. Come out here and park him next to me when you are done. We'll discuss your ride."

Linda turned in a sharp spin towards Taylor and me. I almost jumped back when she started handing out directions. "Taylor you're up next. Head into the arena and grab the headset from Tiera. I need you to run Star through a few lead changes on the rail. Get her warmed up first." Linda's sentences started and ended abruptly, but nearly ran together.

I chimed in as Star walked off. "What do you

need me to do, Linda?"

Linda handed me a ten dollar bill and nodded her visor-topped head towards a white shed surrounded by picnic tables. "I really need a latte." She blurted the statement like it was a life or death situation. "Can you get me one from the food stand? Skim milk, extra shot, one pump of vanilla."

"Sure. A latte it is," I replied, stuffing the crisp bill in my pocket and repeating her order in my head. I didn't know a latte had so many ingredients.

Situated on top of a grassy mound, the snack-shack had a perfect view of all three arenas. From the latte line, I analyzed the horses and their riders – from a safe distance.

The farthest arena looked to be a warm-up pen for halter horses. The muscular animals trotted around next to their handlers and, when asked to halt, squared up their legs on command. The middle arena was packed tight with pleasure horses, loping slow and steady, but the arena closest to the snack-shack interested me the most - gamers, cowhorses, and reiners.

The horses in the third arena turned fast, ran hard, and stopped harder. The riders chatted as they loped next to each other and, for the most part, they were outfitted in jeans and baseball hats. I pictured Casey riding Rocky in that group – we'd been apart for half a day and I was already missing him like crazy.

Ten minutes later and hot latte in hand, I strolled down the hill, walking slower than usual so I could watch the horses.

Two girls walking in front of me slowed their pace too.

"He's so cute," one girl whispered enthusiastically to the other and giggled. Their ponytails bounced in unison as they scanned the arena. I didn't think they were looking at the horses.

"And, I heard he's single again." Both girls squealed.

Although I wasn't interested in their chatter, I quickly figured out who they were talking about. Along the rail came a boy, loping at a good pace on a bay horse. He looked to be about my age, dressed in dark wranglers and a black button-down. He tipped the rim of his cowboy hat and flashed his dimples at the two girls as he rode by.

Serious amounts of giggles followed and I caught myself rolling my eyes at their response. The girls continued walking and gossiping, but I stopped to watch. It wasn't the boy I was impressed with. It was his horse.

His horse's dark mahogany bay coat gleamed

like freshly polished wood and emphasized his muscular build. His jet black mane floated in the wind, the ends skimming the boy's jeans as they loped along in perfect harmony. His mane had to be three feet long - like a knight's horse in a renaissance movie.

As they rounded the end of the arena, the bay horse picked up his pace across the diagonal. He stretched his frame, lengthening his neck before practically sitting in the sand and gliding into a sliding stop. Dirt sprayed out from under his feet like an ocean wave and he left 15 feet of straight hoof tracks in the ground behind him.

I sucked in a breath. Wow. He was beyond gorgeous.

I could have watched for hours, but my fingers started to burn, reminding me of the steaming hot latte I was holding. I rotated it to my opposite hand, cursing the thin paper cup separating my fingers from the boiling liquid. I needed to get back to Linda before I suffered third-degree burns.

But, as I turned to walk off, I met a sharp wave of dirt which ricocheted off my body. I froze in my tracks and caught the end of a perfect sliding stop from the corner of my eye...just a few feet in front of me.

Whipping my head around, I confirmed the identity of the horse and rider – the team I had just watched in awe. I shot my meanest glare towards the boy, knowing he saw me standing just feet from the fence, and I brushed off the front of my shirt. Little pebbles of sand fell to the ground and, as my eyes followed them, I realized the plastic top of Linda's latte was covered in arena dirt too. *Oh no. Not good, not good.*

I blew the dirt off with a quick breath and wiped the lid with the bottom of my shirt. I examined the white plastic, looking for any evidence of filth.

"Sorry about that," the boy shouted towards me, now trotting his horse in my direction. The bay horse stopped obediently at the fence and the other riders rode around him. "Didn't mean to get you dirty. Let me buy you another drink." His words came out like an apology, but his smile and dimples screamed of arrogance.

I continued with my mean glare. "You should watch where you're going." A rider with any manners would know not to execute a sliding stop just feet in front of an on-looker.

"I was," he said with a twinkle of his green eyes. "I saw you watching me ride. Thought you wanted a closer look."

I stared at him, stumped for words. This kid was obviously full of himself and expecting me to giggle and fall to pieces in front of him - just like the two girls did a few minutes ago.

"I was watching your horse...not you." *Wow. What a jerk.* But before either of us could mutter another word, I caught a glimpse of Linda approaching.

"There you are, Lucy," she said, walking towards me and holding out her hand. "I thought you ran away with my latte."

I handed over the drink. "Sorry, Linda. I was just..."

Linda continued talking, not allowing me to finish my sentence. "I see you've met Jace."

What?...Jace? I glanced at the boy. He looked as confused as I was.

Linda ignored our lack of words. "Jace, how is Hammer today? Is he stiff from the trailer ride?"

"No, he feels great. Like always."

"Good, good."

I started to connect the dots. Jace was one of Linda's clients. Hammer was the other horse that Tim hauled up from their barn in California. I wiped the mean mug from my face.

"Why don't you head to the middle of the arena and show me his spins," Linda continued and then took a big sip from her latte.

I bit my lip, hoping she wasn't getting a mouthful of sand.

Swallowing, Linda turned to me, squinting her eyes. "Did you order me a hazelnut latte?"

"No. It's skim milk. One pump of vanilla. Extra shot." I cringed inside.

Linda licked her lips and then shrugged her shoulders. "Hmmm. Tastes a little nutty."

Jace chuckled. "I think that's the snack-shack's signature drink. Right, Lucy?" And he winked before trotting off.

I kind of wanted to punch him.

SIX

Taylor

I lifted the reins and Star smoothly transitioned from a canter down to a walk. I bent over her withers and rubbed both sides of her neck, giving her a massage as we walked through the packed arena.

"You are a superstar," I cooed, pleased with our ride. It was practically perfect.

Exiting through the gate, I sat extra tall in the saddle and felt the crowd's eyes on me - it felt good. *That should give my competition something to grind over. We are going to kick some butt at this show.*

I scratched Star's withers with my fingernails. She bobbed her head, seeming to agree with me, but I think she just liked the scratching.

"Hey, Taylor. Wait for me." The screechy voice

broke into my happy thoughts and I glanced over my shoulder to find Tiera waving frantically as her horse trotted towards me. She was leaning forward and making kissy noises with her mouth, enticing her horse to speed up, but Georgie only knew one speed - and that was slow.

I could've asked Star to trot and left Tiera in the dust, but I was feeling nice in that second. Besides, I didn't want Star exerting herself after that great ride.

"Are you headed back to the barn?" Tiera asked, as Georgie jogged up next to Star and eagerly slowed to a walk. She didn't wait for my answer. "I'll walk with you." Tiera stared at me with big blue eyes and a bright smile. She was like an overly eager puppy dog – which annoyed me.

"Just watch out for the other riders through this area. It's kind of a mess until we get closer to the barn. Don't run into anyone." Tiera's parents bought Georgie from Linda this past spring. He was a seasoned lesson horse, but Tiera was a green rider. And, I certainly wasn't going to be embarrassed by a newbie.

Tiera snapped to attention, absorbing my warning. "Thanks, Taylor. I'll be careful." She inched Georgie closer as a pack of barrel racers trotted past. Star pinned her ears in protest, but neither Tiera nor Georgie seemed to notice.

"Oh my goodness," Tiera exclaimed with an

excessive amount of energy as the horses trot by. "I *love* those glittery things on their hooves! I need some of those for Georgie...in pink!"

I rolled my eyes. "First of all, those are called bell boots," I explained. "Secondly, Georgie will never move fast enough to need them."

But my explanation didn't make sense to Tiera and she scrunched her petite nose. I decided to change the subject. "Has Linda taken you to any shows this summer or is this your first?"

Tiera broke her gaze from the band of trotting horses. "Oh, yes. She took me to the Pleasure Classic about a month ago. Georgie and I took first place in the walk-trot western pleasure class."

"And?" I asked, when she didn't continue.

Tiera raised her shoulders at my question. "And...I was really happy with our ride?"

"No, I meant what other classes did you ride in?"

"Just the one. That's the only one Linda signed me up for."

This conversation was becoming more work than it was worth.

"All-righty then. Was just asking." I ended our little chat with a forced smile and diverted my eyes away from Tiera while I rolled them again.

The Pleasure Classic was an annual show just down the road from Linda's stable and usually the first show she took her rookies to - for good reason. Only locals showed up and the handful of audience members consisted of proud moms with flashing cameras. It was also the first show I competed at. I rode Linda's retired show horse and cleaned house in every pleasure, horsemanship, and trail class for which I was eligible. I was six years old at the time and my legs were just long enough to fit into the stirrups.

Obviously, Tiera was a slow learner. And, I was done babysitting.

Swinging my leg over the saddle, I dismounted and walked Star into the barn. Tiera followed. Close to our stalls, I caught a whiff of warm bread, reminding me it was lunch time. My stomach gurgled as I marveled at the sight of several subway sandwiches displayed on the table in the aisle. Tim stood close, setting out paper plates, plastic silverware, and napkins. Thank God for Tim.

"You're my hero," I said, as I stopped next to the table and ogled the sandwiches.

Tim's face lit up. "Aw, thanks, Taylor. I do what I can around here. Got to keep this place running like a well-oiled machine. Help yourself when you are ready. I got a turkey-bacon-avocado sub just for you."

"Perfect. Thank you," I said as Tim entered the tack room and opened the cooler, rounding up drinks for the crew. The ice rattled as he searched. "What would you girls like to drink?"

"Coke for me, please," I said and Tiera chimed in with something about chocolate milk. I tuned her out and turned to Star. "Come on Babydoll, let's get you untacked. It's time for your lunch, too."

I took a step towards the cross-ties, but froze as I noticed a shiny bay horse and a tall cowboy walking down the aisle - headed straight for me. The boy's black hat brim covered most of his face as he chatted with Linda, but his smooth stride and lean muscular build were as unforgettable as his horse's beauty.

Jace is here?

My heart immediately bashed against my ribs, hard. I grabbed my chest with both hands trying to muffle the sound, convinced Jace would hear it thumping against my bones. I was torn between running away...or running to him. But, either way, I was certain my feet wouldn't work.

Why is he here?

My breathing was audible and, next to me, Star tensed. She arched her slender neck and snorted, loud. She was reading my body language and convinced I saw danger coming for us. She was right.

At Star's snort, Jace raised his eyes and connected his gaze with mine. *Run, Taylor. Run.*

My feet suddenly shot into motion and Star trotted with me through the open door of her stall. She danced in the bedding, but stayed close to my shoulder, her ears pricked forward, looking for the object of my panic. Every step of Hammer's metal shoes on the concrete increased my anxiety as I realized I had backed myself into a corner.

And then the black hat stepped in front of Star's stall.

"Taylor?" Jace asked, as though he didn't expect to see me here.

At his question, Star jumped and snorted like a dominant stallion. In the stall next door, Chance added to the commotion with a high pitched whinny.

Jace seemed startled by his welcome. "What's with Star?"

I took a quick breath. "Nothing. She's fine," I replied abruptly and ran an unsteady hand down her neck. "I think you scared her."

"Sorry. Didn't mean to," Jace responded and offered an easy smile. "I didn't see you in the practice pens."

I avoided his eye contact and focused on unsaddling Star. Hanging a stirrup on the saddle horn, I loosened her girth. "Didn't know you were looking for me."

Jace paused before answering my deliberate statement. "I was. Seems like it's been forever since

I've seen you."

One month and two days to be exact.

"Yeah, well, I didn't know you were coming to this show." I tried to slow my breathing, but felt the hurt bubbling up my throat. "How was I supposed to know you were coming to this show, Jace? Did you forget how to use your phone? Did you forget about me until you got here?" I felt the blood pumping through my body, getting hotter with every word. I pulled the saddle from Star's back and marched through the stall door.

"Here, Taylor," Jace offered. "Let me help you with that."

"No," I responded before he could finish his sentence. "I don't want your help."

Jace stood there, holding Hammer's reins in his outstretched hands, and didn't move an inch as I walked past him. I wasn't sure if his face was plastered with pain or shock.

Pushing past the thick curtain covering the tack stall door, I flung my saddle on top of the rack and then grabbed onto it for support. *Get ahold of yourself, Taylor.* But it wound me up further knowing that I let Jace get to me - again. The heat in my cheeks boiled over into my eyes and I watched teardrops hit the leather on my saddle.

And just when it couldn't get any worse, the curtain rustled and I turned to find Lucy entering the tack room with a couple of buckets.

She stopped with only one foot in. "I'm sorry," she stammered, obviously not expecting to catch me crying. "I...I should've knocked or something. I was just going to get some grain for the horses. I can come back later."

She started to back out as I wiped my tears with my forearm. Just what I needed. This was none of her business.

"Why would you knock? This is a tack room." The words come out harsher than I meant them to and Lucy backed out of the doorway as I stomped through.

Lunch no longer smelled good. I'd lost my appetite.

Lucy

Chance nickered as I pushed open his stall door and crept in, halter in hand.

"Want to stretch your legs?" Chance had his hay spread across his stall floor, but he walked right to me and bumped my arm with his nose. "I know, I know. Sorry. You've been stuck in this little box all day while I took care of everyone else." I patted his forehead. "Now the horses are fed and tucked in for the night. And, we have a little time to play."

I felt more comfortable leading Chance through the barn now that it was quiet. Most everyone had retreated to their trailer or hotel to rest up for the night.

I walked down the aisle and Chance followed, cautiously watching me as we passed stalls filled with horses. They were all dressed in clean sheets and munching on their dinners.

"A little less scary without all of the commotion, huh?" I asked Chance and rubbed him on the shoulder.

Outside, there were a few riders still working in the practice arenas but the far pen was empty. The sky glowed with peach tones - the last bit of sunlight for the day - as I pulled the metal gate shut and unclasped Chance's lead.

He stared at me, unsure what my gesture meant.

"Go ahead," I urged and shooed him away with a few flicks of my hand. "Stretch your legs, big boy."

And with that, Chance hopped to the side and took off in a spurt of bucks which turned into a gallop. His head held high, he circled the arena - but he wasn't running in panic. He was playing.

What a difference this was from the first time I lunged Chance. Then, he ran in fear, pulling the rope out of my hands as he leapt away from me. Now he frolicked in the arena, kicking and snorting and having fun.

Relaxing, I sat in the dirt, pulling my knees to my chest and watching Chance exercise himself, getting his penned-up energy out. He really wasn't made to sit in a stall. I needed to make an effort to exercise him as much as possible while we were here - to keep him from going crazy in that little box. Maybe tomorrow night I could saddle up and ride. It was pretty peaceful this time of night.

As I contemplated the next evening, Chance trotted a few more laps and then made his way to me.

The air was cooling off and the last bit of sun had disappeared behind the trees. Chance reached his head down and I kissed his outstretched nose, wishing I could bottle this moment.

Chance's hooves clip-clopped through the barn as we explored the other aisles on the way back to his stall. Ears pricked forward, Chance was just as curious as I was.

The aisles were filled with color. Each stall was draped in fabric (just like Linda's) which displayed farm colors and logos. Severson Farms, The Jones' Stables, Rick Reedy's Ranch. Everyone seemed quite proud of their own name.

And, there were no naked horses. Every horse we passed was dressed from head to toe in a sheet and a hood. It was hard to evaluate any of the horses when all you could see were their eyes and feet. Although, I was certain they were all gorgeous and expensive.

Tomorrow they would each be unveiled, shined up and ready to perform. I couldn't wait to watch.

Finished with our outing, Chance and I headed back to Linda's area of the barn. But as we turned the last corner, I jumped, not expecting to run into anyone. But there, in the middle of the aisle, was Tiera. She stood with her back to me. Well, she was *kind of* standing.

Tiera had one foot planted flat on the concrete, but her opposite leg was pulled straight in the air, parallel to her petite body. Her hand held her ankle in place and the toe of her tennis shoe was delicately pointed to the ceiling.

I didn't know a person's body could bend like that. I knew mine sure couldn't.

I led Chance on, cautiously, both of us nearly tip-toeing along the cement. I didn't want to scare Tiera as she looked like she was lost in her own world.

As we neared, Tiera released her leg and turned her body into a blur of spins, propelling herself with her own weight, her hands posed in the air like a ballerina on a jewelry box.

Then she stopped mid-twirl, surprised to see me too. "Oh...Hi, Lucy," she said as she regained her balance and pulled the tiny white earbuds from her ears. "I didn't know you were still here."

"Sorry, I didn't mean to sneak up on you like that," I said, leading Chance into his stall and noting that Georgie's door was wide open. The big gray gelding stood obediently in his heavily bedded stall, half asleep and content with going nowhere. "I just took Chance out for a little exercise before turning in for the night. Is there anything I can do for you? Is Georgie okay?"

"Oh, he's fine," Tiera noted. "My Mom and I just stopped by because I forgot to grab my show clothes for tomorrow."

Standing in the middle of the aisle with no makeup, black yoga pants and a simple hooded sweatshirt, Tiera looked younger than I had thought she was. I really hadn't spoken to her today - other than watching her ride in the practice pen.

I tried to make small talk and break the silence. "Do you dance?" It seemed like an obvious question to ask.

Her face lit up. "Yeah, I just started this past year, but I've been learning ballet, tap, jazz, everything. I want to try out for the dance team when I start high school next year."

"Sounds fun," I noted, admiring her eagerness. "All of the balance and flexibility you get from dancing must really help with your riding."

"Yeah, that's what my Mom says, too." Tiera played with the strings hanging from her hood and then dug in her pocket, pulling out a peppermint for Georgie. Georgie perked up when she opened the plastic wrapper, but he waited for Tiera to come to him. He gently lapped the sweet out of her hand and Tiera patted him on the forehead.

Georgie could be the calmest horse I'd ever met.

"All right, Tiera. I've got a copy of your riding pattern for your horsemanship class tomorrow," a petite woman announced as she approached. I looked her up and down and there was no doubt she was Tiera's Mom. She was a brunette version of her daughter - same button nose, same ice blue eyes. They even had their hair styled in the same tight bun positioned at the nap of their neck.

"You must be Lucy," she said, holding out her hand. "I'm Amber, Tiera's Mom. Linda said she had a new helper for this show. Nice to meet you."

"Nice to meet you, too," I responded, shaking her hand.

Amber immediately peeked into Chance's stall. "Is this your horse?"

This time my face lit up. "Yes, this is my boy, Chance." I ran my hand down his neck, beaming with pride.

"He's gorgeous," she said and my heart swelled. "Did you meet our Georgie?" The slender woman practically skipped over to Georgie. She grabbed his nose with her hands and kissed him straight on the muzzle. "He's our baby. Right, Tiera?"

"Yep," Tiera responded and gave him another peppermint. Georgie's gray lip crinkled as he took the treat. He seemed used to the doting. It was pretty cute.

"He seems like a really good boy."

"Oh, he is," Amber cooed. "Well, Tiera, we better get back to the hotel and get some sleep. Big day tomorrow. Did you grab your show clothes from the tack room?"

"Got them," Tiera said and pointed to a thick garment bag laying over one of the chairs. Amber nodded and closed Georgie's door.

"Good night, Lucy," they both said in unision. Tiera waved to me with a smile.

I smiled back, realizing I had judged her too harshly. Tiera may be a bit of a princess, but at least she was a nice princess. "See you tomorrow."

It was 10:00 when I finished brushing Chance and gave him an extra flake of hay. It was time to go to sleep, but I dreaded crawling into bed as my sleeping quarters were in Taylor's trailer - the couch in her living quarters to be exact.

I had no problem sleeping on a couch. I just didn't like the idea of sleeping in the same trailer with Taylor. It was like letting my guard down in enemy territory.

The gravel parking lot was dark, but it was hard to miss Linda's massive trailer on display in the first row. The six-horse trailer with full living quarters rivaled the length of a semi-truck. Her name and barn logo were painted on both sides. The living quarters' lights were still on and I could see Linda and Tim, gathered in the kitchen, chatting and sipping red wine together. They looked like a cute couple.

Next door, Taylor's trailer looked small - only in comparison to Linda's - and I didn't see any lights on. Reaching for the door, I pulled the handle slowly until it clicked open. I tried to make as little noise as possible as I stepped inside. If Taylor was sleeping, I certainly didn't want to wake her up. She was not the nice princess type.

Inside, my eyes adjusted to the dark and about popped out of my head as I looked around. Taylor's trailer may have been smaller than Linda's, but her parents didn't skimp on any luxuries for their daughter. I don't know why I was surprised by that.

The trailer was dimly lit by the glow of a flat screen TV which hung on the wall and faced the queen-sized bed, tucked in the goose-neck of the trailer. Taylor was snuggled up amongst a mob of pillows and fuzzy blankets, zonked out. I hadn't seen her since our run-in this afternoon in the tack room. I had no idea what her tears were about, but I was glad she was sleeping and we could avoid the subject. Communication was not our strong point.

The rest of the trailer looked like a small apartment – a tiny version of a glitzy penthouse. The kitchenette was filled with stainless steel appliances and mahogany cabinets, finished off with a table for two. And, my "bed" was a smooth burgundy leather couch. A folded blanket and fluffy pillow were set on one of the cushions.

Well, that was nice of her.

I set my duffle bag on the floor and sifted through it to find my pajamas. Pulling off my jeans and sliding into my oversized cotton t-shirt, I felt the day wearing on me and sleepiness taking over. A big yawn almost swallowed my face and I about jumped out of my skin when I heard a phone ringing. My phone ringing. And, it was loud.

Oh my God. Where did I put my phone?

I frantically dug through my bag, pulling out pieces of clothing, magazines, a hair brush - trying to find the phone so I could stop the ringing. Five seconds felt like five minutes before I grabbed my phone out of my jean pocket and immediately picked it up.

"Hello?" I whispered with my hand cupped over my face.

"Lucy?" A confused voice asked. "It's Casey. Are you there?"

Casey? My heart jumped a beat.

"Hi Casey. It's me. Sorry, I'm whispering because I don't want to wake-up Taylor."

And, just like that, Taylor sat straight up in her bed, pulling the satin sleep mask from her eyes and glaring into my soul. "Do you mind? Kind of hard to get any sleep around here with you banging around and chatting it up."

She looked at me like I had been jumping on the couch and screaming at the top of my lungs.

"Um, Casey, can I call you back in the morning?"

"Sure, no problem," he responded, trying to hide the disappointment in his voice. "Sweet dreams, Lu."

"You, too." I said, forcing myself to hang-up. I really wanted to talk to Casey. I wanted to tell him all about my day...about the beautiful barn, the horses, and my time with Chance tonight. But, the look on Taylor's face made me close my phone and turn the ringer to vibrate. "Sorry," I noted as I crawled onto the couch and pulled the blanket around me, cocooning myself.

Taylor threw her body down on the bed with a dramatic sigh and I reminded myself she was the reason I got to keep Chance. I committed to working with her – actually, for her – this weekend and I needed to bite my tongue.

I opened my phone once more to send Casey a text, but there was already a text waiting for me.

SORRY TO CALL SO LATE. JUST MISS U. NOT THE SAME AT RRR WITHOUT U.

I smiled, despite the situation, and my body melted into the soft leather couch as I texted him back.

YOUR VOICE MADE MY NIGHT. MISS U TOO.

SEVEN

Taylor

I INHALED THE sweet scent, closing my eyes as I swallowed a swig of hot mocha. The whip cream coated my throat and the heat warmed my fingers, slowly waking my mind. Thank God for mochas. Thank God for caffeine. It was the only thing keeping my eyes open. If I could, I would curl up inside the warmth of this cup right now and fall asleep.

I shuffled down the barn aisle, the soles of my boots skidding along the concrete. I spent most of the night wide awake as my mind raced back to Jace. I just couldn't zone out. I couldn't get him out of my head. And every thought of Jace only increased my frustration.

A month ago Jace flat-out dumped me. He dumped me and never said one word why. He never called me again. He never returned one of my text messages. He dismissed me from his life without giving me a reason.

Who does that?

A jerk. A jerk does that...a jerk I thought I loved does that.

When I laid eyes on Jace yesterday, I was amazed I didn't punch him square in the face. I probably should have. I think that would've made me feel better.

Taking another gulp of warm, chocolaty liquid, I imagined Jace's stunned reaction as my knuckles cracked against his nose.

"Dreaming of something good, Taylor?"

I stopped my feet and opened my eyes at the sound of Linda's voice. "Kind of," I said with a shrug, watching her over the plastic top of my mocha.

"You look like crap," Linda noted without hesitation.

"Well, good morning to you, too," I replied, squinting my eyes in protest of her remark. I pulled the black sunglasses from the top of my head and placed them on my nose. "Just didn't sleep well," I added in a half-growl. "I'll be fine when the caffeine kicks in."

I'd make myself fine. Jace was not going to throw me off my game. I would not let him affect my riding.

Linda studied my face. Even with the dark sunglasses, she knew something was off. She nodded over her shoulder to the stalls. "Go spend some quiet time with Star and get your head back inline. Star is bathed and should be dry by now. She will need to get brushed out and then you can saddle her up." Linda patted me stiffly on the shoulder as she walked past. "There's fresh fruit and doughnuts set out on the table. Get something in your belly other than a mocha."

"Okay," I obliged, grabbing a banana from the table and feeling like I got a dose of mom-advice.

I walked to Star's stall and glanced at my watch as I pulled open her door. Two hours until my first class. I needed to snap out of it.

"Hey there, Babydoll." The words came out in a raspy whisper and Star turned her head to me, presenting a big mouthful of green hay. I moved closer and pressed my cheek against her withers, closing my eyes and breathing in her scent. Even through the fruity shampoo fragrance, I could still smell the wonderful aroma of horse.

It smelled like home. It was all I needed to feel better.

"Already dry, huh?" I asked, still pressing my

body against her soft coat. "Linda is such a pro at bathing horses."

I picked my head up and stood back, scanning her chestnut coat from nose to tail. Not a spot of dirt. Her blaze and socks were the color of fresh snow and her coat a shiny penny.

I smiled.

But my happiness faded as obnoxious giggling rattled through the barn aisle. It was too early for giggling.

"You saved me, Lucy." Tiera laughed through her words as she appeared in front of Star's stall leading a wet Georgie. "Oh, good morning, Taylor." She continued chuckling. "You'll never guess what happened."

Her perkiness was about to send me over the edge. And, I didn't want to guess. "Was it super funny?" I emphasize the word "super," but my sarcasm was lost on Tiera.

"What?" she asked, slightly confused, but continuing with her story. "Anyhow, I was washing Georgie and I used the whitening shampoo. I got him all soaped up and then went to go find Linda because I forgot which conditioner I was supposed to use. Lucy came by and saw Georgie in the bathing stall covered in purple suds and she started rinsing him off. I forgot that whitening shampoo will turn your horse purple if you leave it on too long!" Tiera kept giggling and I wondered what planet this kid came from. "I mean, can you imagine if I turned my horse purple for the show? Thank goodness for Lucy!"

Speaking of the devil, Lucy appeared in a baseball cap and t-shirt, looking about as soaked as Georgie. "It's no problem, Tiera. That's what I'm here for."

"Yeah, that's what Lucy is here for," I noted, hoping they would both quit talking. "What are you washing your horse for anyhow, Tiera?" Tiera barely knew the difference between a forelock and a tail. I was surprised Georgie didn't turn into a purple grape.

Tiera paused to think about my question. "Well, I thought it would be fun. Plus, I've been hanging out with Lucy all morning. She's been teaching me a bunch of stuff." Her toothy smile returned. "I even helped her wash Star."

My back straightened at her last sentence.

"Excuse me?" I thought Linda washed Star.

My eyes immediately shot back to my horse, reassessing the condition of her coat. I stepped around her to check for any imperfection.

"Tiera's a good helper," Lucy noted and my eyes shot to hers. "Is something wrong, Taylor? Did you want me to do anything else with Star before you saddle her up?" She must have caught the craze on my face – she was more observant than Tiera.

All my frustrations were now bubbling to the surface, uncontrollably. Why did *everyone* like this girl? Everyone wanted to be Lucy's friend. It was like the stars aligned for her, bowed-down for her. Tim liked her. Tiera liked her. Linda probably even liked her now. And, on top of that, she captured Casey's heart while my cowboy dumped me faster than a bag of stinky trash on a hot summer day.

I...Couldn't...Stand...Her.

I brought Lucy here to show her a thing or two - to let her know she wasn't as good as she thought she was. And now she was on my every last nerve. "This is not a play date, girls. This is a show and I am here to win. Please don't use my horse as a training device."

Tiera and Lucy looked at me like two baby deer in headlights. They didn't get it. They didn't understand how important this was to me – how seriously I took my riding. And, I wanted them out of my hair.

I continued my rant. "Tiera, you should be getting dressed anyhow. Hand Georgie over to Lucy. She'll put him in his stall."

Tiera followed my orders, turning on her heels and marching off.

"I'm sorry. I didn't mean to..." Lucy started, but I cut her off.

"The silver on my show saddle needs shining.

84

The aisle needs to be swept. All the horses need fresh, clean bedding in their stalls, and I need you to saddle up Star while I get my show cloths on."

That should keep her busy. I only wanted to share my space with Star right now.

Lucy

I followed Linda down the aisle, carrying a bucket full of brushes, rags, and all kinds of sprays.

"You've got the fly spray, correct?" Linda asked, not looking up from her binder as she walked. She flipped through horsemanship patterns and multiple check lists as we made our way to the practice arenas. Her multi-tasking skills were impressive. I could barely carry a bucket, walk, and talk at the same time.

I scanned the bucket. "Yep, got the fly spray and lots of rags."

"Good," Linda noted. "Hammer has a fit about flies. He will need his legs and face wiped down with some spray soon. And, probably again every couple of hours."

"Got it."

Mental note - Jace's horse is a wimp.

The practice arenas were just as packed as yesterday, but now they were an array of colors. All the riders were decked out in their show clothes. There were bright pinks, flashy purples, neon greens and each color in between. A rainbow bounced along the white fence line and I glanced down at my t-shirt, full of horse snot and dust smears. I wondered how the riders kept their show clothes clean all day long.

Tim stood close to the arena, next to Tiera and Georgie. He waved us over with a smile.

Linda began walking faster. "Tiera, honey. Why aren't you in the arena warming up Georgie?" she asked. I noticed Linda took on a softer tone when she spoke to Tiera.

Tiera answered by dancing on her tippy toes, shifting her weight from one foot to the other as she handed Georgie's reins to Linda. "I really have to go to the bathroom," she whispered, her hand cupped to her mouth like it was a secret.

Linda grumbled a bit and I could see why. Tiera was dressed head to toe in pink – from her cowboy hat to her leather chaps. I wouldn't have expected anything else. But, there were zippers and buckles everywhere.

"You're not going to have time to warm-up Georgie if you run to the bathroom. And, I've got to coach Taylor, too. She is getting ready for her first class right now."

Tiera turned her blue eyes to me. "Lucy can do it. Right, Lucy? Georgie loves you."

"I...I guess I can," I stuttered. "If you really need me to."

Linda was quiet, processing her options, but Tiera never stopped dancing. In fact, her pace increased.

"Okay, okay. Hurry up, Tiera." And with Linda's approval, Tiera ran off, leaving me shaking in my mud-caked boots.

It wasn't Georgie that scared me. He was like an oversized golden retriever. It was the masses of well-trained riders in that overstuffed arena and the multitude of judging eyes in the crowd – that was what scared me.

I swallowed the spit in my mouth as Tim took the bucket from my hand. "I'll be the groom for a bit, Lucy. Go ahead."

And, in one short minute, Linda had the stirrups lowered and I was in the saddle - a very expensive, stiff saddle.

Linda tapped her hand on my knee. "Nothing fancy. I just want you to walk and trot around the ring until Tiera gets back."

Nothing fancy? I wasn't planning to do flips off Georgie's back out there. I just wanted to blend in and survive.

She continued. "Georgie is lazy. If anything, you will have to push him forward with your legs. Just get him loosened up. I'll be back after I check on Taylor. Okay?"

"Okay." Her directions were simple enough. I swallowed again but there was no spit left in my mouth.

"You look good up there, kid," Tim said. I had a feeling that Tim told everyone that.

"Thanks," I managed to squeeze out, as Georgie and I walked off towards the arena gate.

"Just follow the flow of traffic," Linda instructed.

Follow the flow of traffic? This was like rush hour in the city. Who was I supposed to follow? I almost had to close my eyes as Georgie and I merged into the mess, hoping I wouldn't collide with anyone.

Horses were nose to butt and moving at all speeds, all directions. And, I felt like Georgie and I were going to be used as a speed bump if we kept walking at his turtle pace.

I clucked my tongue and squeezed my legs, but Georgie just kept moving along at one mile per hour. I squeezed harder. "Come on, Georgie. Let's trot," I pleaded as two riders scooted around us at a lope. The last girl made an effort to sigh loudly as she passed.

I tried one more squeeze and then gave the gray gelding a quick kick with my heels. The kick broke Georgie out of his day dream and reminded him that he was supposed to be working. He hopped up into a smooth jog almost to say, "Oh, is that all you wanted?"

Horses weaved around us while animated trainers and parents yelled instructions from outside the arena. I tried to steady my breathing as we jogged along the rail and was thankful I was on an experienced horse. Nothing rattled Georgie. Georgie had been to a thousand horse shows and he was happy plodding along, doing his job. If I had been riding my horse in this mess, Chance would've fed off my anxiety and fallen to pieces.

My hips swayed side to side in a slow, hypnotic motion and, as we lapped the arena, the gelding's rhythmic trot managed to take the edge off my nerves. It was enough to take my eyes off of Georgie and assess the riders around me.

Trainers shouted directions about keeping heels down and shoulders back, but I thought every rider looked picture perfect. They were like equitation Barbie dolls balancing flawlessly on their shiny horses. My gut tightened as I realized I stuck out like a sore thumb.

As we neared the gate, I was thankful to catch a glimpse of Tiera walking towards the arena, still tucking her blouse back into her pants. She waved wildly and then gave me a big thumbs-up. At least she thought I was doing a good job.

I pulled back on the reins, asking Georgie to walk, and I quickly realized he was much more motivated to slow down than he was to trot. Instead of slowing, he stopped, right in the flow of traffic.

Before I could react, Georgie had started a domino effect.

The girl behind me grabbed her saddle horn as her horse jumped to the side, flattening its ears and narrowly avoiding a crash into Georgie's plump rump. Then there was a blur of shouts consisting of "whoa" and "what are you doing" and "watch where you are going." The yelling came from inside and outside the ring and only reinforced my thoughts of feeling like an outsider.

"Sorry," I squeaked, giving Georgie a swift kick. "Sorry." It was all I could think to say as we scooted out of the mess and through the gate. I hopped off Georgie and handed his reins back to Tiera, wanting to hide my face. I could've caused a wreck.

"I do that all the time," Tiera said as she put a foot in the stirrup, acting like it was no big deal. "Georgie is a fast stopper." The smile never left her face as she settled into the saddle. "Thanks for warming him up. You going to watch my class?"

My heart was still beating in my ears, but Tiera had a way of reminding me that this was supposed to be fun. Horses were supposed to be fun, not stressful.

I managed a smile back. "Yes, of course I'll watch you."

"Okay, follow me," she said, and clucked to Georgie.

EIGHT

Taylor

FROM THE SECOND I glanced at the horsemanship pattern this morning, I knew it would weed out most of the riders in my class. There were quite a few advanced maneuvers in today's pattern, but I loved a challenge. And, Star and I were more than ready.

In the middle of the arena, where it was just me and my horse, I felt every eye watching my every move. I fed off of it. I lived for it...the attention, the pressure. Star did too. It only pushed us to perform at our best.

As one unit, Star and I sashayed down the center of the arena at a slow collected trot with a flawless transition into an extended trot. I barely moved in the saddle as I asked for a lope and then cantered through a figure-eight shape, executing two smooth lead changes and then a pin-point stop in front of the judges. Applause erupted and I nodded at the judges as Star and I walked off.

My pride only grew as I passed the other competitors, lined up on the far end of the arena where they had just witnessed my ride. Their fake, limp clapping and concerned expressions made me smile. They knew I had just won the class.

And, that I had. I patted Star's neck with enthusiasm as the announcer called out my name. "And, in first place for the amateur western horsemanship class, Taylor Johnson and her horse, Obviously A Star. Great ride, Taylor."

I leaned down to take the ribbon from the ring steward, thanking him, and clipped it to the side of Star's bridle. The cobalt blue color popped beautifully against Star's copper coat.

"You sure do look good in blue," I said, as we started our victory lap around the arena. I waved at the crowd even though the stands were only half full. I couldn't wait until Sunday's evening classes when the audience would be packed.

I breezed by the stands, but a sharp whistle caught my attention. Following the noise, my eyes shot towards a certain cowboy, clapping slow and loud. Jace rose to his feet as I loped by. He tipped the edge of his black hat without breaking his gaze and the two girls sitting on the bleachers behind him gave me a dirty look.

I patted Star on the neck and loped on, soaking up everyone's applause. Even Jace's.

I buckled the belt around my waist, running my fingers over the round crystals that covered the leather. Leaning close to the full length mirror, I double-checked my makeup and rolled bright red lipstick over my lips. Satisfied with my work, I admired the entire teal and tan outfit, watching the multitude of crystals bounce light off the glass.

Bling. Bling. Oh how I loved my new western pleasure outfit.

Ripping the tag from the sleeve cuff, I grabbed my matching tan cowboy hat, the brim lined with a teal accent, and opened the trailer door, ready to head back to the barn.

I skipped down the metal trailer steps, still high on my wins from this morning. Star and I were on a roll. If we kept up this pace, I would definitely be in line for the Northwest Stock Horse Championship Title. I nearly squealed at the thought!

"Hey, Taylor. Wait up."

I turned towards the greeting and my heart

skipped a beat. Jace was jogging towards me, making his way through the parked trailers. What did he want? I wasn't ready to talk to him - especially right before my next class.

"I don't have time to talk, Jace," I said, turning my head away from him and walking faster.

"Just give me one minute," he said, grabbing hold of my arm. "Just one minute. I promise. Please just listen for one minute."

His touch was light, his words almost pleading. I couldn't imagine what he wanted.

"What?" I stopped in my tracks, crossing my arms over my chest. "What do you possibly have to say to me, Jace?"

Even with my harsh stance, he didn't let go of my arm. "I wanted to say congratulations on your rides this morning. You and Star were perfect out there. You looked gorgeous...you always look gorgeous."

Jace's emerald green eyes were soft. The tough guy confidence was gone. Truly, I just wanted him to wrap his arms around me and say he was sorry for breaking my heart, but I couldn't give in just like that.

"And?" I asked, not allowing my sudden weakness to show through.

Jace put both hands on my arms now, facing me head on. I looked up at him, trying to look right through him.

"And, I miss you," he said.

His quick words ripped apart my defenses. I looked away, but couldn't bring myself to move from his hold. "What do you mean you miss me?" I asked. "After I left Linda's barn for Red Rock Ranch, I never heard one word from you. You dropped off the face of this earth. And now you miss me?"

"I'm an idiot, Tay." Jace's use of his nickname for me nearly made my knees buckle. "I didn't know what to do. For some reason I thought it would be easier to make it through the summer if we didn't talk, if we took a break. I couldn't stand not being with you...so I thought it would be easier to just stop."

I searched his eyes and the dark features of his face for a real answer, but I couldn't find one. His words seemed sincere, but I just didn't understand his logic.

Jace continued. "And then I saw you here at the show and I knew I was idiot. I miss being with you."

It felt like the wind had been knocked from my lungs. I didn't know what to say. Jace had hurt me - deeply - and now he was in front of me, telling me he missed me?

"I've got to get to the barn, Jace. My class is in 20 minutes."

Jace took the cowboy hat from my hand and gently placed it on my head, adjusting the brim to just the right spot. I didn't uncross my arms.

"I'll be watching from the stands, Tay."

And with that, he walked off. I didn't know whether to be happy or mad. I couldn't tell if Jace had just apologized or if he had just threatened to rip my heart apart again – if given the chance.

Lucy

Chance pushed his black nose against the stall's metal bars, nickering softly and staring at Star.

"Aw...you have a soft spot for her, don't you?" I said and snuck a quick kiss on his whiskered muzzle. He kept his brown eyes pointed towards the chestnut mare as she stood obediently in the cross-ties, ignoring his nickers. I smiled. "Just keep trying to woo her, Chance. I'm sure she'll give in one of these days."

Walking towards Star, I went through a mental checklist, making sure I had everything ready for Taylor's next class.

Saddled up using the teal blue saddle pad. Check.

Tail brushed out and fluffed. Check.

Fly spray wiped on with a rag. Check.

I dug into my pocket for a carrot piece, but when I extended my hand, Star nuzzled the orange bit in my palm, analyzing it like I could be feeding her poison.

I chuckled. "You can take it, Star. It's just a vegetable, I swear."

She sniffed the mystery treat a few more times before delicately picking it up with her lips.

Chance nickered again, this time for me. "I've got one for you too, buddy. Don't worry."

I dug another piece from my pocket and handed it to Chance. He lapped it up before he even knew what it was.

"I'll be waiting outside by the arena." Her voice made me jump. "I need some fresh air before my class."

"Taylor," I said, clenching at my heart. "I didn't even hear you coming." I was half-afraid she was going to yell at me for giving her horse a treat, but she just walked by. She looked like she was in a trance. Maybe she was tired. Or maybe she was in her zone, concentrating on her next class.

"Thanks for getting Star ready."

I paused, wondering if my ears heard Taylor correctly. I didn't know her vocabulary included that word.

"You're welcome." The words came out like a question. "Do you need anything else for your class?"

Taylor responded over her shoulder. "No, I'm fine."

But something was definitely not fine. Something was off.

"All right. I'll bring Star out by the arena in a few minutes."

Tiera and her Mom took off for the afternoon, noting a mother-daughter day at the mall, and Jace's classes were done for the day. Taylor's western pleasure ride was the only class left and I wanted to watch. I tidied up our area of the barn, sweeping the aisle and organizing the tack stall before sneaking off to the arena, anxious to watch the class I had been hearing about all day.

Grabbing the first open seat I found in the bleachers, I settled in for the show.

"Please enter the arena at a jog," the announcer stated in a smooth, even tone. "After two tough cuts, this is the final cut in our open western pleasure class here at the Northwest Stock Horse Championship Show. Good luck to everyone."

Following the announcer's instructions, the horses and their riders entered the arena through the far gate, one by one, and they meant business. Their straight faces emphasized intense concentration as their horses jogged slowly, in single file, along the rail.

Taylor and Star were the last team to enter the arena before one of the show volunteers shut the gate with a clang. As always, they looked perfect, not a hair out of place. Whatever was bothering Taylor before had obviously been forgotten.

The announcer continued. "Class is complete. Please continue at a jog."

You could have heard a pin drop. I sat still, afraid I'd move and cause the bleachers to creak, breaking the tension hanging in the air.

"And, lope your horses."

At the announcer's request, 20 horses transitioned into a lope. There were four judges dressed in navy blazers and khaki pants, scribbling notes on their clipboards as the horses passed. My eyes darted from one horse to the next, trying to find a fault in any of them. I couldn't. This was the best of the best and everyone was here to win.

"Extend your lope."

The riders barely moved as they asked their horses to pick up the pace. Taylor and Star loped by, in perfect form, but as they passed, I thought I saw her shift her weight quickly in the saddle.

That was odd.

I kept my eyes glued to the pair as they rounded

the next corner and Taylor seemed to lose her seamless equitation position, leaning forward and then suddenly grabbing the saddle horn with her free hand.

My hand shot to my mouth and I gasped, realizing what was happening. The girth was loose. Star's girth was coming undone and the saddle was falling to the side.

I stood up in the stands, my hand still cupped to my mouth, as the saddle slid off-center and Star's head shot straight up. Not understanding what was happening, Star scooted her butt underneath her belly and shot forward into a bucking spree. Taylor pulled on the reins, trying to stop her, but by the time Star hit the middle of the arena, the saddle and Taylor went sailing through the air, hitting the ground in a unanimous thud. The audience inhaled at once, making a giant sucking noise, as Star continued to buck, her reins now flailing at her sides.

The two judges at the far end of the arena put their hands in the air, yelling "whoa" and trying to control the escalating situation as other horses were now joining the fiasco, prancing and hopping in circles.

"Please halt your horses," the announcer demanded, the tension now audible in his voice. A few of the riders dismounted, feeling safer on the ground.

Star let out one last kick before slowing to a trot and stopping to snort. With her ears pricked forward and neck arched, she looked as stunned as the audience and her confusion gave one of the judges just enough time to grab the hanging reins.

With Star now under control, every head turned towards her dismounted rider. Taylor was sitting in the dirt with another judge kneeling by her side and she looked to be brushing him off, shaking her head. They both stood and a small group of audience members clapped, trying to show support.

A couple of the horses started to prance again. "Please hold your applause," the announcer warned and the arena became silent.

Taylor walked, a bit stiff, towards Star and took her reins from the judge. She didn't brush herself off. She didn't say a word. She walked past every stare, leaving her saddle and her bent cowboy hat in the dirt.

I watched her exit through the gate before I took off in a sprint, running past the murmuring audience. And, as soon as I hit the open air, I spotted Star. Walking next to Taylor, the chestnut mare's head was now lowered, looking ashamed at her irrational reaction.

"Taylor," I called after her and jogged to her side. "Are you okay?"

Without taking the time to stop and properly roll

up the ends of her chaps, the soft tan leather scrapped across the ground, dragging through the dirt with each stride. She didn't look at me. I knew she was upset.

"Would you like me to take Star back to her stall for you?" I figured there was something I could do to help. Taylor probably needed some time to herself.

"Get away from me, Lucy," Taylor said through gritted teeth. "And, don't ever touch Star again."

"What?" I asked, baffled at her response. "I was just trying to help..."

Taylor turned on her heels, forcing me to an abrupt stop as she pointed a finger straight at my nose. "Help? *HELP ME?!* Don't you think it would have been *HELPFUL* if you had tightened the girth when you tacked up my horse?" The corners of Taylor's brown eyes were crinkled up in anger while her finger stayed pointed at my face.

My mouth dropped open as I stared at her, without words. Taylor was blaming me for her fall? She was putting the blame on me after I had followed each and every one of her bratty instructions since we got here? Not to mention, I did *NOT* forget to tighten Star's girth. I know I checked it before handing Star off. I wasn't stupid. Who did Taylor think she was?

Instead of biting my tongue, I snapped.

"Why didn't *you* check the girth on *your* horse,

Taylor?" The words bubbled out of my mouth. "That's an elementary horse lesson – to check the saddle before you put a foot in the stirrup." The blood pumped faster through my veins with each word, sick of her know-it-all attitude. I wasn't taking the blame for something I didn't do.

Taylor's lips pressed together in a thin, straight line as she digested my reply. There was dirt ground into her red lipstick.

"I paid thousands of dollars for you to come here to work and you can't even tack up a horse correctly. I don't even know why I brought you here."

A crowd was gathering around us.

I balled my fists together, keeping them close to my sides so I didn't smack her. "Why did you bring me here, Taylor?" If I was going down in flames, I might as well get some answers. "Did you bring me here to rub your money in my face? Because I am not impressed."

A brief wave of shock shot through Taylor's eyes before they hardened and she spit out her response. "I brought you here because I felt bad for you, Lucy. I felt bad for you and your pathetic horse and I thought you could learn something here - make yourself a better rider. Or, maybe teach your horse some manners." Taylor paused, feeding off the situation's drama. "Obviously, I was wrong. I learned my lesson. I shouldn't associate myself with someone who is going nowhere."

Her words came out in a low hiss, hitting me at my core like a punch to the gut. I stood motionless as Taylor turned and walked away, seemingly happy with my reaction.

How could anyone be so self-centered? So wrapped up in her own world that she didn't care who she hurt? My feet started to back up as I felt my throat constrict. I needed to get out of there before I let her see me cry.

NINE

Taylor

I WALKED AWAY as fast as I could - so fast that Star jogged to stay by my side. I was pissed. I thought about running, but I wasn't going to give Lucy the satisfaction.

Star's metal shoes clip-clopped against the concrete floor as we navigated the barn. I narrowed my eyes at a tall guy pushing a wheelbarrow and he quickly moved to the side, out of my way.

Back at the stalls, I came to a quick halt. I wanted to untack Star and get the heck out of there before I had to deal with anyone. I reached for Star's bridle and she jumped away, looking at me like I had hit her.

Star glared at me, eyes wide open and ears

pricked forward. Her body leaned away from my outstretched arm.

She thought I was mad at her.

I dropped my arm, letting it rest against my side as I lowered my head. I concentrated on slowing my breathing. "I'm sorry, girl," I whispered, taking a deep breath. "I'm not mad at you. I promise."

I was mad at Lucy. I was mad at myself for letting the whole thing happen.

"It's okay," I said and repeated the words over and over. I reached out slowly and Star allowed me to rub her neck. She seemed to accept my apology as she let her body relax.

"Taylor." Jace's voice cut through the thick air. He was slowing to a jog as he approached. "Are you okay? I can't believe that just happened."

Neither could I. And, I didn't want to see anyone right now – especially Jace. I wanted to be alone after taking a roll on the arena floor. How embarrassing.

"I'm fine. I'm fine," I said, brushing off his question. I was fine...physically, anyhow.

"Let me help you, Tay." And Jace didn't wait for me to answer. He grabbed Star's halter from her stall door and took the reins from my hand. I didn't have the energy to fight him. And, in a few seconds, Jace had Star's bridle off and clasped her nylon halter behind her ears. He turned back to me and it felt like something snapped inside my heart.

I wasn't sure if the feeling came because I just flipped off my horse and smacked the ground, or if it was because I had been disqualified from a class I should have won, or if it was because my ex-boyfriend was standing in front of my face confusing the heck out of me...whatever it was, I'd hit my breaking point.

"I'm not really okay." I pushed the words out as a lone tear rolled down my cheek.

Jace stepped over and wrapped his arms around my shoulders. His touch sent me over the edge. Cradled in his familiar scent, I pressed my head against his chest and let my tears soak into his shirt. He rubbed my back with his hand and let me cry in silence.

But, I didn't let myself cry for long. It was embarrassing enough that Jace had to witness me like this. I didn't want to stand here and wait for Linda and Tim to find me. Straightening up, I swiped my face with my crystal encrusted sleeve, wiping away the tears and choking back the rest.

"How about I keep you company while you cool off Star. It looks like she could use a walk and a bath."

Jace's emerald eyes waited for my response.

I nodded.

And just like that, Jace handed me Star's lead

and wrapped his arm around my back. The three of us walked out of the barn, together.

Lucy

I had to take a walk. What I really wanted to do was run to Chance and bury my face in his mane, close my eyes and forget the words that Taylor had just lashed across my face. But, I knew the culprit would be there, in the barn, untacking Star. And, I knew I couldn't be around her right now. One of us was bound to rip the other's eyes out.

So I power-walked, trying to leave behind the anger, the hurt. I pushed forward, quickly covering ground and making my way down the driveway, away from the barn. When I had no more pavement to follow, I stepped onto the grass and walked beside the white picket fence - towards a little band of yearlings. The youngsters were nibbling at the grass, swishing their short tails in the sunshine, and enjoying each other's company. I plopped down, taking a seat in the grass and resting my head in my hands.

Horses didn't judge. Just being near them gave me peace. Enough to calm me down anyhow.

An hour later, my mental state was somewhat in line and I headed back to the barn - which now felt like enemy territory. I walked down the aisle, looking for enemy number one and ready to retreat if necessary. I didn't know what Taylor would do if she saw me now. And, my stomach felt queasy just thinking about it. She couldn't take back the check she had written for Chance, could she?

Peeking down the aisle, I saw that Star was back in her stall, sheeted up for the evening, and the rest of the crew was gathered near. Linda and Tim were talking, examining Linda's clipboard, as Tiera and her Mom filed out of Georgie's stall, their hands full of brushes. There was no sign of Taylor.

"Hey Lucy," Tiera said, locking eyes with me and waving a curry comb in the air.

Tim and Linda both turned their heads.

"There you are," Tim said. "We were starting to get worried about you." Had Taylor told them I was responsible for her fall? Would they believe my side of the story?

"Sorry. I was watching a few of the classes and time just got away from me." It was the first thing I could think of.

"Well, we are all headed to a dinner tonight. The show committee puts it on every year. There's a big buffet. Would you like to join us?" No one was showing any signs that they knew about the fight between Taylor and me.

"Actually, I'm not that hungry." It was the truth, even though I hadn't eaten anything since breakfast. I just didn't feel like being social right now - or running into Taylor. "Do you mind if I just stay here?" A quiet barn was what I needed.

"You're going to miss out on the world-class chocolate-chip cheesecake at dinner." Tim licked his lips, tasting it in his mind. "You don't want to miss out on that. Do you?"

"Thanks for the offer, but I was kind of hoping to ride Chance. He's been sitting in his stall all day and I'm sure he's about to go crazy."

At that, Tiera piped up. "Can I join you, Lucy?" She immediately turned to Amber. "Please, Mom. I never get to ride on the trails here because no one ever wants to go. Pretty please, pretty please, pretty please." Tiera pushed her hands together in a praying motion, the curry comb hanging from her wrist by a string.

I didn't even know there were trails around here.

Amber scrunched her delicate face in apprehension, but then looked to me. "Only if it's okay with Lucy. And, you only walk and trot. And, you're back here before sunset."

She had a lot of requirements.

Tiera jumped towards me, raising her hands in

the air like she had already won. "Can I, Lucy? Can Georgie and I come with you on a ride?"

A trail ride sounded like the perfect way to forget my afternoon. And, it would be nice to hang out with someone who actually wanted to hang out with me.

"Sure, Tiera."

She squealed at my approval and jumped around the aisle, doing a little happy dance.

"All right then. You girls be careful while we are gone," Linda instructed as she set down her clipboard. "Tiera, as soon as you get back from the trail ride, I want you to call your mother and let her know."

"Yes, ma'am," Tiera replied with a two-finger salute to her forehead.

Linda continued. "It's just going to be you girls here so stick together. Jace and Taylor went into town for a bit and are meeting us later tonight for dinner."

Jace and Taylor were hanging out? I hadn't seen them say two words to each other.

"Yes, Linda." I agreed with her instructions. I didn't care who Taylor was hanging out with. At least I knew she wasn't going to be here. "We'll be careful. And I'll make sure Tiera calls when we get back."

Taking a breath, I opened Chance's stall. "Okay,

Tiera. Let's get saddled up."

"Thank God for you, Lucy," Tiera exclaimed dramatically as we rode side-by-side, leaving the barn in the distance. "Otherwise I'd be sitting at dinner, forced to listen to boring adult talk."

"Well, I'm glad I could get you out of that." I smiled at her honesty. Tiera seemed unaware of my crappy mood. She babbled on, keeping the conversation rolling and my mind off the knock-down-drag-out fight with Taylor. Tiera was helping me unwind, helping me forget.

I could forget for now, anyhow. There were still two more days left of the show. Eventually I would have to be in the righteous presence of Taylor again, knowing she blamed me for her fall...and basically called me an idiot who couldn't even saddle a horse.

My blood began to boil again, warming my cheeks, so I tuned out of my head and into Tiera's babbling.

"And that's why I hate those stuffy dinners," she said, ending a story I had completely missed, and then turning to see my reaction.

"I see," I said and nodded, responding to her raised eyebrows. "I don't think I'd like that either."

I didn't know what story Tiera had told me, but

she seemed to appreciate that I was agreeing with her. She smirked, but was quickly distracted.

"Oh!" she gasped. "There's the start of the trail!"

I followed Tiera's pointing finger and found the green and white metal sign, hovering above a cluster of sparse bushes. As we rode closer, I could see this wasn't just some dinky trail. We were riding towards the main trailhead of the Central Oregon State Park.

"Wow," I said, slowing Chance to a stop and admiring the squiggly white lines drawn all over the metal sign. The lines connected and made up an extensive map of horse trails. "We could ride on these for days."

"I know!" Tiera squealed. "I've been dying to ride on these trails since we got here, but no one ever wants to go with me. Everyone is so wrapped up in the show."

A grin crawled across my face. "Well, I'm glad you asked me," I said truthfully. It was the first time I felt at ease since I left the ranch. "Do you want to lead?"

"You can lead," Tiera noted and ran her fingers through Georgie's short gray mane. "Chance's strides are so much bigger than Goergie's. I'll probably have to lope to keep up with his trot."

Tiera's smile widened at her comment and I was instantly reminded of her Mom's warnings.

"We better be careful. Remember, your Mom was pretty serious about only walking and trotting." I could just imagine the wrath I'd face if Tiera took a tumble in the dirt. I pictured Amber's petite frame coming completely unglued. I did not need to see that.

Tiera rolled her eyes as Georgie walked by Chance. "Blah, blah, blah. My Mom worries if I eat an apple that's not organic. Trust me. We'll be fine." And with that, Tiera gave Georgie a little kick and they loped off towards the trailhead. "Come on," she yelled, waving her hand at me without looking back.

I shook my head at Tiera, knowing I wasn't going to change her mind. But I was thankful for that.

Chance was thankful too. Anticipating a run, he bunched up like a spring and pranced in place before I loosened his reins, allowing him to follow Georgie. We quickly caught up and as soon as we were next to the gray gelding, Chance snorted into the fresh air. The horses loped along with their heads held high, taking in the open space before us.

All four of us were soaking up the freedom, leaving a trail of dust in our path.

I plopped down in one of Linda's chairs,

monogramed with her name, and giggled along with Tiera as we cracked open ice-cold Cokes. Tiera pulled the elastic band from her pony tail and let her white blonde hair fall to her shoulders. She continued to laugh as she ran her fingers through, tugging at wind knots.

"I can't even believe Chance jumped straight over that creek! I can still picture the look on your face!"

"The look of horror, you mean?" I noticed my cheeks were sore, tired from our laugh-fest. "I can't believe I stayed on!"

"You sure he wasn't a jumper before you got him? You guys practically cleared Georgie & me. I don't think Chance got one drop of water on his hooves."

I shook my head and smiled, remembering the scene. "I seriously think Chance spooked at his own reflection in the water. He thought there was a big black monster staring back at him or something. He was NOT going to step foot in there."

Chance was now resting in his stall, eating his dinner and watching us as we laughed. He stared back through the metal bars with a mouthful of hay and snorted in our direction, dismissing our silly chit-chat.

"I know, I know. We'll stop making fun of you," I said, holding back a final chuckle and turning to Tiera. "I suppose I should have expected that. Chance isn't used to sitting in a stall all day long, doing nothing. He had a lot of energy to burn."

Tiera nodded her head to agree. "He needed the ride. Maybe we can try another trail tomorrow? I only have the one class in the morning."

"That'd be great," I said, but quickly remembered the real reason I was here at the show. I took a big swig of Coke followed by a long breath. "As long as I don't have stuff to do here...for Taylor." I caught the disgust in my voice as I spoke her name. I couldn't help it.

Tiera caught it too. "I don't know how you can take orders from her." She didn't know I had no choice. "I'd go crazy. She's so serious about everything. I mean, lighten up already." Tiera picked at the pink nail polish crumbling off her thumbnail. "I'm glad she didn't hang around the barn today. I can't imagine what she'd be like after her fall in the ring today." She looked at me with raised eyebrows.

"Yeah, I can't imagine," I replied, not allowing sarcasm to lace my statement. I knew exactly what she was like, but I hadn't clued Tiera in on the gossip. She didn't know that Taylor accused me of being the reason for her not-so-graceful dismount - or that Taylor and I had screamed at each other, nearly fist-fighting. I didn't want to rehash it. I wasn't going to gain anything from letting Tiera in on the craziness.

I changed the subject. "Poor Georgie must be worn out," I said, not seeing any sign of him through the stall bars. "He's already lying down."

Tiera popped up in one swift movement, abandoning her chair, and skipped across the aisle. "Oh, he's so cute when he lies down." She nearly squealed the word "cute" as she slid open the stall door.

I stood to join her. I agreed - a horse snuggled up in a thick bed of shavings was pretty dang cute. I wanted to take a peek, too, so I approached the open door with slow steps. I didn't want to scare Georgie into standing up. But then again, I didn't think there were too many things that actually scared Georgie.

In the stall, the gray gelding had all four legs tucked up underneath himself, his head and neck raised. Tiera was kneeling in the bedding by Georgie's head, a hand on his shoulder, but she pulled away as Georgie turned to nip at his own belly.

Tiera looked back at me and I caught the fear on her face. "Something's wrong," she said.

I stepped into the stall and immediately noticed the hay on the ground, still in two untouched square flakes. The bottom of Georgie's rubber bucket was covered in grain – which he would normally have lapped up in thirty seconds. His neck was dark with sweat.

The scene in front of me was a horse owner's worst nightmare. Georgie was showing us all the signs of colic.

TEN

Taylor

JACE PARKED HIS car next to Linda's long aluminum trailer. The black leather interior of his cherry red Mustang radiated the scent of his cologne, fresh yet spicy. It filled my lungs and was hard to ignore – just like Jace. Trying not to be obvious, I silently studied his square jaw and chiseled features as he clicked the car key back, turning off the purring motor. He cocked his head towards me and I quickly looked out the windshield, afraid of what would happen if I looked straight into his eyes.

Jace Brooks was two years older than me, a senior at a rival high school in my hometown of Napa, California. But even though we lived in the same town, we'd never met until after he started training with Linda this past year. Believe me, I would remember a face like that.

At first sight, I was stunned by Jace's model-good-looks. Heck, he looked like he could stroll into an Abercrombie photo shoot and steal the show with one wink. But it wasn't his beautiful face or athletic body that did me in. It was his riding. After I watched Jace compete on Hammer, I couldn't stop myself from falling for him. I was fascinated by Jace's intensity and confidence through every perfect maneuver of his reining pattern. I had found the male version of myself – someone who would understand my love of the sport, the competition.

"It was pretty boring driving the 300 miles to this show by myself," Jace broke into my thoughts.

I rolled the seatbelt strap around my fingers, knowing exactly what he was referring to. Before I left for Red Rock Ranch, I had kept Jace's passenger seat warm on the way to a horse show in Vegas. His comment zapped my mind back to the trip - the hours we spent talking, the mounds of gas station junk food we consumed, and the songs we got lost in as they played over the radio.

"We do make a pretty good road trip team." A tentative smile curled on the edge of my lips. "Except that you always steal my Skittles."

"Well, who can resist Skittles?" Jace kidded and cracked opened the car door. "I mean, come on. You can't hold that against me. They're delicious."

Our eyes locked for a millisecond before he winked at me and stepped out onto the gravel. My heart palpated, unsure of why he was giving me so much attention. After all, Jace was the one who had pushed me away. And now he was flirting with me? And, why was I letting him flirt with me? *Be strong, Taylor. Don't let him wiggle his way back into your heart...at least not without getting some answers. And, an apology.*

I stepped out of Jace's car, leaving behind the scent of his cologne and feeling relief as the cool night air hit my skin. But still lost in my jumbled thoughts, I shut the door a little harder than I meant to. The crash echoed off of the aluminum metal of the horse trailer.

"Hey, ease up on the muscles there, Taylor. No need to get in a fight with my door."

I turned around to match his sarcasm with an equally witty comment, but the words never left my mouth as I scanned the parking lot. "Jace?" I called out for him and peeked around the back of his car. His six-foot-two frame had disappeared.

"Up here, Tay."

Following the sound of his voice, I looked to the sky and found his lean build staring back at me from the top of Linda's trailer, a dark silhouette in the dimming light.

"What are you doing?" I asked, amazed at how quickly he got up there.

"Come on." Jace waved his arm at me. "Come up here with me. It's quite the view."

I just spent all evening with Jace. He had walked with me as I cooled down Star and had kept me company as I bathed her. At dinner his attention continued, making me feel like I was the only girl in the restaurant. Looking at Jace from the ground with the sun setting at his back, I knew it was a bad idea to climb up there with him - to give in to him now.

But I did it anyway.

Jace was waiting at the top of the metal ladder as I climbed up the rungs. He held out his hand for mine and I grabbed hold, placing my cowboy boot on the metal roof. "You know Linda's going to kill us when she finds us up here, right?"

He squeezed my hand and then led me over to the square stack of hay bales nestled in the rack. "That didn't seem to stop you from coming up here," he replied with a grin. "Besides, we left dinner early and you know Tim isn't leaving without at least a few pieces of cheesecake." He hopped up on the hay bales and I followed.

"Yeah, you're right," I agreed, very aware he was still holding my hand. "They probably won't be back for another hour or so."

My palms were sweating now, unsure where this

was leading, and also knowing I needed to confront Jace with my questions. If I was going to ask him for answers, this was my opportunity.

"Look," Jace said with a nod of his head, pointing the brim of his black hat towards the practice arenas. "We've got front row seats to check out our competition for tomorrow."

Wiping the palm of my free hand on my jeans, I looked ahead to the dimly lit arenas. The first two pens were filled with tall lanky horses tacked in English gear while the farthest ring held the quick-stopping reiners. I grinned, knowing Jace was just as competitive as I was.

"There are some really great riders here," I noted quietly.

Jace laced his fingers through mine and turned his gaze back to me, flashing a smile. "Nothing you need to worry about, Tay. You and Star are the team to beat at this show."

I chuckled half-heartedly. "Not after my dismount into the dirt today."

"That wasn't your fault. That stuff happens to the best of us."

I sighed, knowing I could have prevented it. "I should have checked the girth. It kind of was my fault."

"Don't worry about it. You were so far ahead on points from your wins earlier today. I'm sure you can make up the difference tomorrow. You'll be back in the running for the championship title in no time."

I stewed over Jace's words for a few silent moments. "I guess I just need to win every class I'm entered in for the rest of the weekend." I smiled. My words were meant to sound sarcastic, but the truth was hard to hide. I wanted to win the title and I was going to do everything in my power to make it so.

Jace didn't respond, but when I looked up, I found him analyzing me, his emerald eyes intense. He set his arm across my shoulders and my pulse quickened, bounding into my throat. I knew what he was doing and I wasn't sure how I should react.

I'd planned out this moment since Jace pushed me away. Since he stopped returning my calls, my texts. I'd dreamt about slapping him across the face and calling him every cuss word I could think of. I wanted to remind him what he lost and how he could never have it back. I wanted to make sure Jace hurt as much as I did. My head told me to push him off the roof of the trailer and laugh when he hit the gravel below.

But I didn't. I let Jace kiss me.

His lips followed mine, slow yet forceful. He tightened his arm around my back, pushing me into his chest, and my hand found the sharp curve of his jaw. The anger in my heart melted away with each second. This was where I wanted to be and where I shouldn't be, all at the same time.

And I nearly cried when he stopped.

"I've wanted to do that since I saw you yesterday," he whispered, just inches from my lips.

Jace's actions in the past 24 hours contradicted everything he had done in the past month. "I don't understand you, Jace Brooks," I said, searching his eyes for a hint of an explanation.

"What's there to understand, Tay," he asked with a flirty smirk.

I started to ask why he was such a jerk, but Jace pressed his lips to mine and my question disintegrated from my brain. Jace knew how to get his way.

Kissing Jace gave me a late night urge for Skittles – sugary goodness in rainbow form – but I wasn't sure where I would find candy at 10:00 on the show grounds. Determined, I pulled on my yoga pants and left my trailer on a sugar hunt. The vending machine by the show office was my only hope.

The parking lot was deserted as I walked towards the barn using both hands to finger-brush my hair into a high bun. Wrapping the elastic tie around my curls, my mind drifted back to Jace...and his kiss. His emerald eyes. His tight grip around my shoulders. His chest pressed against me.

The visions made me sigh.

There was something about him that forced my stomach to flutter, over and over again. I couldn't make it stop. And, after that kiss, I knew Jace felt the same way about me. He knew he had made a mistake and now he wanted me back. But this time our relationship was going to be different. This time I was going to be in control of the situation. I needed to set boundaries, rules. Tomorrow I would sit Jace down, looking especially cute in my breeches, and tell him we could only be together if he was exclusive - my boyfriend. I deserved that. I deserved to know exactly what he was thinking.

I sashayed into the barn, thoroughly impressed with my plan, and headed for Star's stall. She deserved a snack too - a few carrots and some love, especially after today's events.

The aisles were dark, lights off and horses sleeping, so I was surprised to see the lights blazing over Linda's section of the barn. Maybe Tim was checking the horses before bed? But as I approached the stalls, I caught the sound of Lucy's voice and I slowed my stride. Did I really want to deal with her after such a perfect evening? I wasn't in the mood for a buzz-kill.

But before I could turn around, Lucy hurdled

herself out of Georgie's stall, kicking a cloud of cedar shavings into the aisle as she ran straight towards me. I froze.

What in the heck? What was she doing? Did she hear me coming and go completely insane with rage? Was she planning on beating me senseless while no one was around? I weighed my options. Lucy was tall and wiry and definitely faster than me. I couldn't outrun her so I tightened my fists into balls, ready to take a whack at crazy-train. As she got closer I braced myself for a Lucy-style football tackle. Maybe if I tripped her...

"Taylor," she shouted, like she was happy to see me.

"What?" I barked back, realizing my balled fists were now positioned in front of my chest, ready to fight. Not that I'd ever been in a fight in my life.

She skidded to a stop in front of me, nearly wiping out as her cowboy boots slid across the concrete. But instead of slapping, pushing or kicking me, she grabbed hold of my wrist and pulled, hard, taking me with her.

"Ouch!" I squeaked, stumbling a few steps before I was forced to follow. "What is your problem? I'm the one that took a flying leap into the dirt. Remember? I'm the one that should be mad and assaulting you."

Lucy didn't stop pulling, but she did turn her

head to make eye contact while she ran. "Georgie is colicking. This is *not* about you."

My thoughts flipped as I absorbed Lucy's words and grasped the seriousness of the situation. Colic, a stomach pain usually caused by a blockage in the intestines, was not something to mess around with. It could take the life of a healthy horse in a matter of hours.

Realizing Georgie needed my help, I fell in step with Lucy's pace and soon we were running, side by side, towards Georgie's stall. Arriving, I grabbed the wooden edge of the open door to stop myself and Georgie flicked his ears in my direction. Lying down in the bedding, Georgie's soft gray coat was dark with sweat, mostly on his neck and chest. His eyes were droopy, and there were wet marks on his belly where he had nipped at his own pain.

Tiera was standing in the stall with her hands to her mouth. When she turned towards me, her eyes were glassy and I noticed her fingers starting to tremble. I stopped myself from gasping at the sight of Georgie. Tiera didn't need another reason to be scared.

Behind me, something crashed to the floor in the tack stall, and Lucy came out with a halter and lead.

"Tiera," I said, controlling the anxiety in my voice. She looked helpless and had probably never seen a horse colic before. "Where's your phone?"

She patted down her jean pockets and replied, "It's on the table in the aisle."

I stepped into the stall and put a hand on her arm, gripping it firmly. "Here's what I want you to do." Tiera was listening to me with every ounce of her attention. "Grab your phone and run to the show office. There's a list posted on the door with emergency numbers. Call the vet and tell him your horse is colicking. Then I want you to call Linda and tell her the same thing." Tiera nodded. "And tell Linda that Lucy and I are both here and taking care of Georgie while we wait for the vet."

Her bottom lip quivered. "Okay, Taylor," she said before sprinting out of the stall.

Lucy swooped in as Tiera ran out. She knelt by Georgie and quietly clasped a halter over his head. As she stood, Georgie laid his head down in an attempt to start rolling. His legs began thrashing through the bedding.

"We've got to get him up," Lucy yelled. "He could make it worse if he rolls."

I was thinking the same thing and jumped towards Georgie's hind end. "Come on, Georgie. Come on. Get up. Come on, boy." I clucked and waved my arms as Lucy pulled him forward with the lead rope and muttered her own words of encouragement.

Georgie managed to get his feet underneath

himself and groaned as he straightened his front legs. He was trying to do what we wanted him to, but he was hurting.

There was more clucking and kissing and waving of the arms before the other horses realized something was wrong. Star whinnied and Chance pawed against his door. Hammer began pacing back and forth. Everyone was telling Georgie that he had to get up.

"Yup, yup!" I started making sounds like I'd heard Casey and the ranch hands yell during cattle round-ups. I clapped my hands and Lucy and I both held our breath as Georgie made a deep grunt and pulled himself into a standing position.

I wanted to scream for joy, but I knew we were far from being in the clear.

Lucy led Georgie out of the stall. His head hung low, but he was walking.

"We need to walk him until the vet gets here," Lucy said. "God, I hope he hurries." She walked Georgie down the aisle, but it wasn't long before the gelding tried to lie down. His front knees buckled and both Lucy and I started yelling and flailing our arms again.

Georgie walked forward a few steps at our urging. "He's really in pain," Lucy said, the worry on her face increasing. "I wonder if Linda packed any Banamine. Who knows how long it will take the vet to get here and we need to do something for him while we wait."

Banamine, an anti-inflammatory drug used to help relieve pain during colic, was a common medication for horse owners to keep on hand in case of an emergency – just like this one.

"Linda has a bottle in her trailer," I replied. I knew exactly where it was stashed. Last year I watched Linda grab it from her trailer's tack room when her horse, Cash, started showing signs of colic at a rodeo. "But, I don't know how to give an injection. We'll have to wait for the vet or for Linda..."

Lucy cut me off. "I know how to. I took an equine health class a few years ago with my 4H group. Can you go get it?"

Lucy's sudden confidence caught me off-guard, but I didn't hesitate. "Will you be okay by yourself with him for a few minutes?"

"I think so," she said. "Just hurry."

It was a good thing I was wearing yoga pants and tennis shoes because I ran like the wind, bursting out of the barn and across the gravel parking lot. I never ran, but I could have finished a marathon on the adrenaline pumping through my blood. The key pad on the trailer beeped at me as I punched in the numerical code and then swung open the door, jumped in and ripped open a cabinet drawer.

"Gotcha," I said, grabbing the white plastic tote with the Red Cross symbol and tucking it under my arm. I blazed a trail back to the barn and slowed to a jog as I approached Lucy, certain I had set some kind of record. I pulled a syringe and the glass bottle of Banamine from the emergency kit and set the rest of the tote on the ground.

Lucy took the bottle and syringe from me and handed over Georgie's lead rope. "Just keep him still," she instructed.

In a matter of seconds, Lucy filled the syringe with the clear liquid drug and tapped her finger against the plastic to remove any air bubbles. She stepped towards Georgie and placed a hand on his lower neck, finding his jugular vein.

I tightened my grip on Georgie's halter and cringed as Lucy slipped the needle into his neck, but Georgie didn't move a muscle as she injected the medication. When it was all done, Lucy popped the plastic cap back over the needle and placed her hand on Georgie's neck, keeping pressure on the injection site to stop any bleeding.

I was at a loss for words. Lucy knew exactly what she was doing. I'd watched a few injections before, but I couldn't have done that. Lucy knew every step it took to give the shot and she did it with ease.

"Okay, let's walk him again," she said and I

followed her instruction, silently thankful she was here with me. "It shouldn't be long before the Banamine kicks in."

An hour later the barn was a calmer scene. The vet, an older gentleman with silver hair, pulled a business card from the front pocket of his plaid flannel shirt. He handed the card to Linda. "Georgie should be just fine now, but I would suggest watching him for a few more hours. If he starts to show signs of pain again, call my cell phone. Otherwise, I will be back to check on him first thing in the morning."

Linda held Georgie's lead rope as he stood in the aisle, his head slightly raised and his brown eyes perked-up. "Thank you for getting here so quickly, Dr. Kalen. I really appreciate your help."

"That's my job, Mrs. Green," Dr. Kalen said as he packed his stethoscope in his canvas bag of tools. "What really saved Georgie was the quick work of these three girls here." He smiled at Lucy and me and winked at Tiera. "You should be very proud of them."

Tim and Linda chimed in at the same time. "Oh, we are."

I gave a sheepish smile, not sure how to take the praise. Lucy really deserved the compliment.

Bag in hand, Dr. Kalen waved at the group circling Georgie. "I'll see you at six tomorrow morning. Have a good night folks."

As Dr. Kalen walked away, Georgie nuzzled Tiera's pockets, softly searching for hidden treats. He was starting to act like himself again. Tiera laid her head against his neck, releasing a big sigh, and kissed his gray coat.

"All right girls, it's time for you to get some well-deserved sleep," Tim piped up as he gently took Georgie's lead rope from Linda's hand. "Otherwise, you will all be zombies during the show tomorrow and zombies don't usually win their classes. I will set up camp next to Georgie's stall and watch him overnight."

Linda leaned over and planted a kiss on Tim's cheek. "Thank you, Sweetie."

Tiera and her Mom hugged Georgie before Tim walked him into his stall. I snuck into Star's stall to say goodnight to my baby as well, thankful she's never had to fight the pain of colic.

Star was standing against the wall with her back leg cocked and her bottom lip droopy, clearly wanting to fall asleep. I checked each snap on her pink plaid sheet, making sure she was comfortable and safe. Then I kissed her on the nose, holding the kiss a bit longer than normal.

"Sweet dreams, Star," I whispered. And, when I

turned to leave, I noticed Lucy whispering her own affections to Chance. She was running her hand over his forelock and down his nose. My eyes locked with hers through the metal stall bars, but this time there was no hate, no hurt between us. No words were said, but I didn't think they were needed.

ELEVEN

Lucy

"SHE DID IT again!" Tiera squealed over the roaring sound of applause from the audience. She hopped up and down as we stepped back, making space for the arena gate to swing open.

"She sure did," I said clapping my hands together. I was a little less enthusiastic than Tiera, but I was still clapping.

A single row of riders filed out of the arena, all in tan breeches, navy coats, and black velvet helmets. The outfits for the English classes were not nearly as thrilling as the blinged-out western outfits from the day before. These riders looked like a line of clones only differentiated by the color of their horse. And those jackets looked awfully stuffy.

Tiera kept clapping as the horses exited, blurting a positive comment to each rider. "Good job. Nice ride. Love your boots," she said, jumping back and forth on her tiptoes, squeezing her hands together.

I smiled at her honest excitement for each rider and wished there were more girls like Tiera.

As Taylor rode Star out of the arena, her smile spread from ear to ear. Star walked with her head held high, strutting and fully aware they had just won the class.

"I've got the brushes," I said, grabbing the bucket full of grooming tools and fly spray. The plastic tub had become like a purse for me. I toted it around all day, making sure the horses looked their best in the show ring. Today, I was only looking after Star and Hammer as Georgie was on stall-rest, recovering from last night's incident. I was so glad he was okay.

Tiera had to scratch her classes for the day, but it didn't seem to bother her much. Plus, she volunteered to be the assistant's assistant for the rest of the weekend. It was nice to have a helper – especially one with such a great attitude.

I handed Tiera a fresh bottle of cold water. "Can you see if Taylor needs a drink?"

"Absolutely," Tiera said with enthusiasm.

"Need me to do anything else?"

"No, I think both Taylor and Jace are done with their classes for the day."

Tiera nodded and skipped towards Star. I followed, wishing I had a fraction of her energy. I was tired. It had been 1:00 or 2:00 in the morning before I finally drifted off. I'd tossed and turned trying to get situated in my bed - the leather couch in Taylor's trailer - but I was amped up from the colic scare. And, Taylor was acting really strange.

Last night Taylor was unusually quiet as we walked from the barn, following Linda to the trailers. And as we put our pajamas on and crawled into bed, she clicked on the flat screen TV and asked me if there was anything I wanted to watch. I stared at her without words from the couch before she handed me the remote. She didn't toss it. She didn't throw it at my head. She handed it over with the tiniest of smiles and then got situated in her quilted comforter.

"Watch whatever you'd like," she said. "Good night."

I was frozen on the couch waiting for some kind of sarcastic comment to follow. When it didn't, I wondered if a few drops of the Banamine drug had soaked into Taylor's skin, making her loopy. That was my best guess as Taylor had never made an effort to be friendly to me - not since we'd met. Was I being punked?

And then her friendly behavior continued today.

Taylor reached down from the saddle and took the water bottle from Tiera, unscrewing the cap. "Thank you," she said before tilting her head back and finishing off every drop. "It's so hot today. I feel like a sweaty mess. I'm glad I can get out of these clothes now."

Taylor popped down from the saddle and patted Star on the neck before handing the empty bottle back to Tiera. She didn't look like a sweaty mess at all. In fact, I was convinced her body was not capable of perspiration. She looked as clean and crisp as she did this morning - not a hair out of place or a dirt smudge found anywhere on her outfit. I, on the other hand, was a sweaty mess.

"Do you want me to take Star in the barn and untack her?" I asked.

Taylor pulled her gloves off, finger by finger, and nodded. "Yes, that would be great, Lucy. Thank you. I'll be in the barn soon. You can leave her in the cross ties and I will walk her out."

I took Star's reins and wondered who this person was. Maybe the Banamine went straight to her brain and scrambled it.

Taylor unclipped the chin strap on her helmet and pulled it off as she walked away, exposing her neat blonde bun. Her hair didn't know what helmet-head was either.

"Well, she's certainly in a good mood today," Tiera said, as she gave Star a peppermint. Star crunched it in dainty bites.

"Yeah," I replied. "Does that seem weird to you?"

Tiera shrugged. "Kind of, but wouldn't you be in a good mood if you just won three classes in a row?"

Tiera was right. I was analyzing Taylor's behavior too much. Taylor was doing what she loved – winning. Why wouldn't she be happy?

"Plus there's *that* whole situation," Tiera added and I followed her wide-eyed gaze to find Taylor lip-locked with Jace. Her hands were wrapped around his neck, the velvet helmet dangling from her fingers.

"Well...I should've seen that one coming," I said, a little stunned.

Tiera and I stood, our heads cocked inquisitively, watching the act in front of us unfold yet knowing we should look away. Jace's hand gravitated down the back of Taylor's navy blazer and I grabbed Tiera's arm, pulling her towards the barn.

"Come on," I said. "I don't want to witness Jace grabbing a handful of breeches."

Tiera spun with me and walked while still examining Jace & Taylor over her shoulder. Her gaping mouth told me I had been right about the breeches.

Tiera giggled about our piece of gossip as I clipped Star into the cross-ties. "Oh my goodness! I can't believe Jace and Taylor were making out! What if Linda or Tim saw them? I mean...are they supposed to do that?" Her eyebrows rose at her own question.

I set Star's lightweight English saddle on a metal rack in the aisle. "Well, I don't think it's illegal or anything," I said, as I shrugged my shoulders. "But, I don't think Linda or Tim would be very happy if they caught them. That was pretty ballsy of Taylor to go in for the lip-lock right next to the arena. I mean, we practically saw their tongues."

Tiera wrinkled her nose and put her hands on her hips. "Gross."

A chuckle slipped out of my mouth at Tiera's reaction to the witnessed kiss, but I muffled it as I noticed Linda, Tim & Amber making their way down the aisle.

"Do you think we should tell them?" Tiera whispered, covering her mouth with her hand.

I instantly shook my head back & forth. "No, it's none of our business." Truthfully, I just didn't want Taylor back on my case. It was nice not having to worry about her tantrums.

Tiera nodded knowingly and zipped an imaginary zipper across her lips.

Linda stopped at the table and set down her binder full of show papers. She had an unusually big smile plastered on her face. "Now that's the way to start off a show day," she noted with a head bob. "All blues for both Taylor and Jace today. If they keep this up, one of them is bound to snag the championship title."

"Green Stables is unstoppable," Tim chimed in with a jolly hurrah. "And, why wouldn't we be? We have the best riders, the best horses, and the best assistants." He winked at me and Tiera.

"And, of course, we have the best trainer," Amber added, putting her arm around Tiera's shoulders and looking at Linda.

"Well, that goes without saying," Tim said before he kissed Linda on the cheek.

I cleared my throat to break through the love-fest. "Linda, Taylor said she wanted to walk Star and cool her off herself." I brushed Star's back to wick away the sweat left by the saddle. "What would you like me to do?"

Linda looked around. The floor was spotless and everything in its place. "Why don't you take a break, Lucy? Star & Hammer are done for the day. Enjoy a few hours off before you need to feed the horses their dinner. Tim and I are going to watch some more classes in the indoor arena and Amber is taking Tiera shopping downtown for a new dance outfit."

Tiera hopped in place at the mention of a new dance outfit.

I was grateful for the suggestion of a break, but I didn't really know what to do with myself. "Okay. Are you sure there isn't anything you need me to do?"

"Not a thing," Linda said. "Why don't you ride your own horse? The reining classes are done in the big outdoor arena and it shouldn't be too crowded out there this afternoon. It would be a good place to exercise Chance."

And, as if he heard his cue, Chance pawed twice at his stall door. His brown eyes stared at me, certain I was talking about him.

"Yeah, I like that idea," I said. Chance bobbed his head up and down at my voice. It looked like Chance liked that idea, too.

I brushed Chance in his stall while I waited for Taylor to arrive and, by the time I had him saddled, she strutted into the aisle. She was humming something unrecognizable, but upbeat. Her cheeks were pinked and she spun her helmet in lazy circles around her fingers.

"I wiped down your saddle and bridle and put them back in the tack room," I told her from Chance's stall.

Taylor jumped like I shouted my statement from the rooftop and then nervously laughed at herself, putting a hand to her chest. Chance jerked his head up at her reaction, watching her like a hawk.

"Oh, wow. I didn't know anyone was still here," she said with a giggle.

I analyzed the strange sound I heard coming from Taylor – laughter – and then I continued. "I wouldn't leave Star standing in the cross-ties by herself. You never know what could happen."

Taylor took a breath and shook her head. "No, I wouldn't expect you to do that. Thanks for taking care of her."

Was that a compliment?

"That's what I'm here for," I said slowly, waiting for a back-handed comment to follow.

Taylor unclipped Star from the cross-ties. "Are you taking Chance for a ride?"

Was she really interested in what I was doing?

"Yes," I replied, unsure how to act around this new, uncharted version of Taylor.

"Great," she noted as she started leading Star away. "Have a good ride."

Chance and I peeked our heads out the stall door

to watch Taylor and Star walk away. Taylor went back to humming and twirling her helmet. And, there was an extra sashay in her step. I didn't take my eyes off her as she led Star out of the barn.

"Let's just enjoy this while it lasts, Chance. She's bound to implode at some point."

I double-checked Chance's girth before I raised my knee to my chest and put a boot in the stirrup. That same precaution may not have occurred to Taylor, but I certainly didn't need another reason to end up flying through the air. I had enough of those.

As I situated myself in the saddle, Chance began to prance in place, having too much energy to be patient. I rubbed his neck with my hand and tightened my grip on the reins.

"Easy, boy," I cooed to him. "I know you are sick of standing around in that dang stall. The weekend's almost over and soon we'll be headed back to the ranch where you can run around in the pastures and hang out with your buddies. I'm sure Sharkie and Rocky are missing you." I knew I was missing the ranch...and, without a doubt, Casey.

Chance flicked his black ears back and forth listening to my story, but he didn't stop prancing. "Okay, okay," I said and gave him a gentle squeeze with my legs. My calves barely brushed his sides before Chance marched forward into an energetic walk. "Let's go find this outdoor arena Linda was talking about."

Earlier today, Jace won his reining and cutting classes in the outdoor arena, but I hadn't laid eyes on the ring yet. I stayed close to the barn and the indoor, making sure Taylor and Star were taken care of. After all, Taylor was the one who wrote me the check and the real reason I was here. Not to mention, there was something about Jace that rubbed me wrong. I made sure his horse, Hammer, was always taken care of, but I didn't go out of my way for Jace's sake. He could focus his big-headed ego elsewhere. One princess was plenty to take care of.

Walking away from the barn and past the practice arenas, I watched the riders from a distance as they moved gracefully in circles. Watching them, my mind flashed back to the panic I felt while riding Georgie in the warm-up pen and I secretly hoped the arena I was headed towards was deserted. Georgie was the sweetest, easiest-going horse I knew and I still almost caused a crash. I physically shook the memory from my head, not wanting to tense up and freak Chance out.

"Let's have a good ride. Okay, Chance?"

Chance marched with vigor as we followed a short dirt path towards a barrier of tall pine trees. In the middle of the trees there was an opening framed by two tall wooden posts, topped with a rustic sign. The sign was engraved with the words "Welcome to the Rodeo."

I liked the sound of that.

Passing through the gate, my eyes widened at what the trees had been hiding. The outdoor arena, as Linda called it, was a huge oval arena about the size of a football field. Empty wooden bleachers wrapped around the sides and the far end was made of metal bucking shoots - for the rodeo broncs and bulls. An announcer's stand rose above the metal shoots like a white cottage. A massive American flag hung from the rectangular open window on the front of the stand.

The setup looked like it came straight out of the Wild West. I couldn't wait to ride in it.

I clucked and Chance hopped into a stretchy trot aimed for the open gate. He seemed as excited as I was to try out our new-found adventure. And, we had it all to ourselves. Even better.

I posted Chance's big trot as we entered the arena and he stretched his neck to the sky, surveying our new surroundings. The dirt was freshly tilled. Only a few lines of hoof tracks left circles on the ground. Three metal barrels painted in red, white and blue stripes were strategically placed in a pyramid form.

They must be running barrels in here later this evening.

I pictured the white bleachers filled to the brim with a cheering crowd, the announcer's raspy voice blaring over the speakers, and a dark night sky brightened by the glare of the arena lights. I pictured the crowd's eyes on Chance and me as we raced around each barrel at lightning speed. It was a beautiful sight.

A grin spread across my face and Chance lengthened his trot, checking out the barrels in front of him.

"What do you think, Chance? You want to try running a pattern?" I whispered my question like it was a secret.

What the heck. No one is here to see me if I screw up. Who cares if I knock over a barrel or two.

Following my impulse, I directed Chance towards the first barrel on our right and he followed my cues. I giggled as he slowed down and jogged a tear-shape around the metal obstacle.

"Good boy," I praised him before aiming his nose at the second barrel on the left side of the arena. Getting excited by our new game, Chance broke into a canter. I didn't stop him. I just adjusted my body to the faster speed, knowing he had energy to burn.

We neared the second barrel and Chance started to turn towards it before I asked him to. He loped another perfect tear-drop shape and I leaned forward in the saddle to follow his motion. But my movement seemed to click something in Chance's head and he proceeded to kick himself into high-gear. Chance dug deep into the dirt, his front end rising like a speed boat accelerating through the water. I grabbed the saddle horn, surprised by his enthusiasm, but I was just as anxious to run as he was. I gave him the reins to go.

With ears pricked forward, Chance locked his eyes on the third barrel and I leaned into his neck. His body stretched out underneath me. And when we came to the third barrel, Chance turned with such intensity that we leaned together at a 45 degree angle, breezing around it. I grabbed the middle of his thick black mane and moved with him as he exploded towards the gate we had entered, not even 30 seconds ago. The wind nipped at my face and blew through my hair – just like a new question flew through my mind. *Where did that come from?* Chance circled that last barrel like he'd been running them all his life.

Nearing the gate, I sat back in the saddle and pulled Chance to a controlled canter just as I realized we were being watched. Immediately, my body stiffened.

"Whoa, Chance," I said, as I tightened the reins and rode him into a circle, barely missing a collision with two riders. They must have come in right after me.

Chance started to trot, showing his irritation for the slower speed by tossing his nose in the air. After another circle, he gave in and came to a stop, blowing a loud snort through his puffed nostrils. My legs involuntarily bounced against his ribs as the air left his lungs.

Halted, I was facing the two riders and their horses. Both of the girls' brows were scrunched up, looking mildly confused as they observed Chance and me. After a few seconds of uncomfortable silence, the brunette girl on a big bay horse spoke. "Did you just get here or something?"

Her question sounded irritated and I thought about my answer before responding, not knowing what she was getting at. "What do you mean?"

The second rider, a petite red-head on a lanky palomino, chimed in. "Did you just get here? We haven't seen you riding in the practice pens."

"Oh," I responded as Chance blew out another snort. "No, I've been at the show for a couple of days."

The girls pursed their lips together, still staring at me. I wasn't sure what they wanted so I continued, just trying to fill the silence. I asked them the same question. "Did you guys just get here?"

"Um, no," they said in unison, sounding

offended.

"Who's your trainer?" the brunette asked bluntly and then turned to her friend. "Her trainer was probably riding her horse in the practice pens and that's why we didn't notice her." She was very sure of herself.

"Well, I don't really have one," I replied.

"What do you mean you don't have a trainer?" They both blurted, again in unison, and I wondered if they had some kind of telepathic communication.

"I don't have a trainer," I repeated. "I train my horse myself."

The girls looked at each other and started to laugh. Their bodies shook against their shiny saddles and that's when I noticed that they were both wearing black baseball hats embroidered with a trainer's name. Obviously they had a trainer, but why did they care if I had one?

"You're kidding, right?" the brunette said as she cocked her head. "Everyone has a trainer. I mean, everyone who counts has a trainer."

The girls snickered again and my patience grew short. Who did they think they were? I felt like knocking their matching hats off their big heads with a swift blow.

But before I could respond to their snickers, a voice from the fence broke into our conversation. "Not everyone has a trainer, Sandra." The statement was very matter-of-fact.

All three of us turned to look over our shoulders and found Taylor sitting casually on the top board of the arena fence. She was no longer in her show clothes, now wearing jean shorts and holding a soda. Star was only a few steps away, grazing on a patch of lush green grass. She wasn't exactly the person I wanted to see lurking in the shadows.

"Oh, hey Taylor," Sandra, the brunette, said as she sat up straighter in her saddle. I guess Sandra wasn't excited to see Taylor either. "I didn't see you there."

"No kidding," Taylor noted and continued in a cool tone. "Like I said, not everyone has a trainer. And, *some people* like to pay their trainers to do all the work with their horse...and *those people* think they can take all the credit when they win." The girls started squirming in their saddles and Taylor hardened her gaze. "How do you like your new horse, Sandra? Isn't that the gelding your trainer won the National Finals Rodeo Championship Title with last year?"

Taylor's words sounded sweet to the ear, but they were laced with disgust. She took a long, slow gulp of her soda, letting her questions sink in. "It sure is nice to have a rich daddy. Isn't it, Sandra?" Taylor finished her rant with a wink.

Sandra and the nameless red-head looked like

they had been caught stealing cookies out of the cookie jar. They glanced at each other and rode off without another word. There was no snickering as they left.

I wasn't the target of Taylor's rant, but I was speechless just the same. Taylor, the girl who looked down her nose at me, who bossed me around, who blamed me for her nose-dive into the dirt...this same Taylor just had my back?

As I sat there, stunned, Taylor spun her tan legs over the top of the fence and hopped down to the ground. She walked over to Star and started braiding her flaxen tail as the chestnut mare continued grazing. I rode Chance over to the fence and watched Taylor expertly weave the thick braid and wrap a rubber band around the end.

I wasn't sure I should be thankful for Taylor's tongue-lashing skills, but I appreciated being defended. Instead of a thank you, I said the next best thing. "Congratulations on your wins today, Taylor. You and Star make quite the team in the show pen."

A brief smile graced Taylor's face. "Thanks," she said and ran a hand over Star's muscled rump. She patted the mare a few times and then turned to face me, crossing her arms. The intensity in her hazel eyes had me wondering if I was her next victim.

"Don't let them treat you like that," she instructed. "Don't let anyone talk to you like that.

You don't deserve it." My mouth must have dropped open because I felt it drying out as she continued. "Those girls could never ride a horse like Chance. They win because mommy and daddy buy them horses that are broke to death. And when they start losing because their skills can't keep up with their horse's talent, mommy and daddy just buy them a new horse."

I couldn't believe the words that had come out of Taylor's mouth. In her own way, she had given me a compliment on my riding - the thing I held closest to my heart. I watched her as she picked-up Star's lead rope from the grass and started to walk off.

"Taylor," I called after her. She stopped, looking at me over her shoulder and waiting for my response. "Thanks."

She gave me a nod and continued on. Maybe I didn't know Taylor as well as I thought I did. Maybe I didn't know the real Taylor at all.

TWELVE

Taylor

MY POINTER FINGER flew down the list of names, nearly smudging the black ink as it dried on the paper. The official show rankings had been updated and posted just minutes ago as the last class of the day was now complete. Finding my name under each class I competed in, I tallied the numbers in my head. For each ribbon won, I earned a certain number of points and I was hoping I was still a contender for the all-around championship title. My stupid nose dive into the dirt could've screwed everything up.

I was halfway through the list when one of the show volunteers walked out of the office armed with a single piece of white paper. As she started positioning the new paper on the corkboard, it dawned on me what she had – the point *totals* for each competitor.

I watched her out the corner of my eye, trying to appear casual, but wanting to rip the results from her hands. I just about screamed as she took her time placing a thumbtack on each corner of the paper, making sure it hung straight.

Happy with her work, the volunteer pushed the last tack into the corkboard and walked away. As soon as she turned her back, I leaped the distance to the other side of the board, ready to devour the new information.

"Come on, come on, come on," I muttered to myself as my eyes focused on the list. My hands involuntarily clasped together at the suspense, but a squeal quickly escaped my lips as I found my name. I was in second place with one more day left of the show! I still had a shot at the championship!

My feet danced around in a little jig as I pictured Star and myself posing for our magazine shot, standing proudly next to our new saddle and golden trophy. "Yes!" I meant to whisper the word, but it came out more like I'd just completed a touchdown. I balled my fist together and jerked my arm down by my side in a celebratory thrust. However, in my celebration, I didn't notice that someone was sneaking up behind me...until my elbow connected with their flesh.

"Umph," a voice gasped into my ear and I spun around to witness Jace doubled over with a hand on his stomach. "Geez, Taylor," he said as he looked up at me. "I wasn't expecting to get pounded for trying to give my girlfriend a kiss."

"Oops." I shrugged my shoulders, but I didn't feel too bad. I was still celebrating in my head. "Don't be so sneaky next time," I instructed, half-kidding and half-serious.

At my comment, the sparkle returned to Jace's emerald eyes and he gave me a one-sided grin. "You are quite the handful, Taylor Johnson." His playful smirk was infectious and I felt my lips turning up in a grin.

"I could say the same of you," I replied, liking how he called me his girlfriend in the midst of getting elbowed in the stomach. And then I remembered why I got so wound up in the first place. "Guess who's in the top two of the point standings so far." I raised my eyebrows and cocked my head, challenging him to say anyone else's name but mine.

Jace walked towards me with slow steps and took my hips in his hands, pulling me closer. "Me and you," he said before dipping his head down and grabbing my lips with his.

Normally, a kiss from Jace would give my body

tremors and send my heart into an uneven rhythm, but his three words shocked my system. They weren't what I was expecting him to say. My eyes froze open and my lips wouldn't move with his kiss. After a few seconds, Jace pulled back.

"Is something wrong?" he asked, looking a bit offended.

"What did you say?"

"Tay, I asked you if something was wrong."

"No." I shook my head. "Before that. What did you say before that?"

"I said you and I are the top two contenders for the championship title. I called the show office about ten minutes ago for an update." His smile widened again. "Isn't that great?"

The realization of Jace's statement sunk in...Jace was in the number one spot. I was behind him in second place.

"Oh," I said, making sure my face didn't fall as I gently broke out of his hold. "Yeah, that's great." I turned away, not so gently, to get a better look at the list.

Sure thing. Jace Brooks' name was at the top of the list, above mine, and beating me by five points. My body went numb as Jace put his arm around my shoulders, smiling and oblivious to my reaction.

I didn't know how to feel. On one hand, Jace was now my boyfriend, something I'd wanted for months. I should probably be happy for him, show him support. That's what girlfriends were supposed to do. On the other hand, he was the only thing keeping me from taking home the Northwest Stock Horse Championship title, an award I'd worked so hard for, wanted with every fiber of my body. And on top of that, I surely would have been in the number one spot if I hadn't botched up my western pleasure class with a stupid loose girth.

Jace turned his head towards me and gave my shoulders a quick squeeze. "Pretty exciting. Right, Tay?"

In that moment, I was thankful for my years of rodeo-queen experience. I flashed my best plastic smile and nodded my head while my insides screamed.

Jace kissed me again. "I'll see you tonight at the bonfire, right?"

"Yeah, for sure," I said with all the enthusiasm I could muster. Every muscle in my face tightened to force another grin.

Jace pulled me into a half-hug and winked as he turned away. My eyes followed him as he walked, but my mind was clouded with calculations. I had two more classes tomorrow, both of which Jace was also competing in – mountain trail and the freestyle horsemanship class. He'd be tough competition. But, if I could win both classes, I would earn enough points to take home the championship award.

I folded my arms across my chest, wondering what Jace's reaction would be if I beat him. What would my reaction be if he snagged the title from my hands? Neither of us liked to lose, but there could only be one champion.

I was beginning to wonder if there was any way I could win – whether I took home that champ saddle or not.

Star's head popped up as I approached her stall and she blew out two soft nickers at my arrival - nickers meant only for me.

"Hey there, Babydoll," I said, reaching through the metal stall bars and picking a single strand of hay from her flaxen forelock. Star batted her long, black eyelashes as I ran my fingers down her forehead to the soft fuzz of her nose. "Make sure to get your beauty-sleep tonight. We've got some serious butt-kicking to do tomorrow."

And, as though she understood the seriousness of my whispers, Star reached for her hay net with vigor. She chomped her teeth around an excessively large chunk of hay and ripped it from the nylon net. She tossed bits through the air with a few flicks of her nose, showing the hay who was boss.

Her aggressive approach to eating made me chuckle. "Now that's the kind of sass I like to see."

Just as Star settled from her hay-beating, my ears caught the sound of oats rattling against plastic. Star heard it too, and a few seconds later, Lucy emerged from the tack room, four feed pans stacked on top of one another. Her arms were wrapped around the balanced heap.

All four horses whinnied in eager anticipation.

"Hey, Taylor," Lucy greeted me with a timid smile. Her chestnut ponytail was peppered with hay bits. I felt the need to pick them out.

"Hey," I responded as she walked towards me. "Which pan is Star's? I can give it to her."

"That'd be great. Her grain is in the second pan." Lucy stood still as I took the top two feed pans off her stack, taking Star's and rearranging the other pan back on the pile.

Pushing open Star's stall door, I set the plastic feed pan on the ground and Star dug in. As she ate, I watched Lucy distribute the rest of the grain. Across the aisle, she fed Hammer and Georgie, patting them each on their foreheads before closing their doors. As she walked towards Chance, he nickered in the same soft tone that Star had just greeted me. Lucy rolled open his stall door, whispered a few words and then held his grain pan against her chest. Chance lapped up the oats and watched Lucy as he chewed.

He gazed at her like she deserved his full attention.

I cleared my throat. "So, how long have you been practicing barrels on Chance?"

Lucy turned her head, looking surprised by my question. I thought it was obvious small-talk after witnessing her run barrels in the outdoor arena. She raised her shoulders slightly. "I've never practiced barrels on Chance."

"What?" I asked. The word shot out of my mouth. "You've *never* practiced a barrel pattern with him? No way."

"No, I haven't. I promise." Lucy raised her shoulders higher like she was shocked herself. She whispered her next sentence like she was afraid she'd done something wrong. "That ride in the outdoor arena was the first time I've tried him on a barrel pattern."

I chuckled, but it wasn't meant to be condescending. It was a stunned chuckle. "No way," I restated. "He ran that pattern like he knew what he was doing." I would have accused Lucy of lying, but I knew she wasn't capable of it.

She glanced back at Chance as he licked up the last pieces of grain. "I honestly don't know where that came from. It was like something clicked in his head when we turned around the second barrel...like he knew what he was doing."

"Something clicked?" I asked. "Like a memory?

I didn't think he was broke when you and Casey found him. I mean, I saw him explode and toss you through the air like a wet noodle." Lucy gave me a small smile and I knew she didn't take offence to my comment. I wasn't being rude. It was the truth. Chance went rodeo-bronc-crazy the first time Lucy got on him. And, I was pretty sure he did it a few times after that.

"I really don't know much about Chance's past other than he came from Billy Jackson's place." Her eyebrows wrinkled sharply at Billy's name. "And I don't think Billy was running barrels on Chance. He couldn't even get close enough to put a halter on him. I'm certain he didn't even like horses. The cops told us he inherited a bunch of them from his Dad."

"Maybe his dad rode Chance?"

She shrugged again. "From the picture the cops painted of Billy's dad, I think he was more of a horse trader than a rider. I'm thinking he picked Chance up at an auction somewhere hoping to resell him and make some money."

"Maybe Chance had some training before he ended up at the Jackson's?" There had to be an answer to this puzzle. Chance didn't learn those moves on his own.

"It's possible, but I'm not sure I'll ever know his full story. It's not like I'm going to call up Billy and ask him for the details."

"Yeah, he seemed pretty shady," I responded, remembering Lucy's confrontation with Billy at the Cowboy Race's awards ceremony. In particular, I remembered the way Lucy screamed at him, and the fear covering her face.

"'Shady' might be an understatement," Lucy noted as she closed Chance's stall. From her tone I could tell there was more to the story, but Lucy didn't offer it up and I didn't press the issue. "Is Star all done with her grain?"

Star was already mowing down on her hay and I grabbed the grain pan from the stall floor, handing it back to Lucy. She did a good job of looking after the horses. She obviously cared about all of them – not just her own horse.

"You've got Chance's registration papers, right?" I asked, thinking I could probably help with a piece of Chance's puzzle.

Lucy gathered Hammer's and Georgie's feed pans and responded over her shoulder. "Yeah, I've actually got his papers in my duffel bag in your trailer. I've been meaning to Google his sire and dam..."

I didn't let her finish. "I can do better than that."

THIRTEEN

Lucy

I FOLLOWED TAYLOR into her trailer and watched as she grabbed an iPad from the kitchen table. She plopped down cross-legged on the leather couch, as the tablet screen came to life. She started tapping before looking up. "You just going to stand there?" she asked, raising her eyebrows and then giving a pat to the leather with her hand.

I was still standing in the doorway. "Oh," I noted. "Guess I could take a seat." It was hard to forget that this was Taylor's space. I felt like I needed to respect that. But...she was technically sitting on my bed.

I walked over and took a seat opposite Taylor. "So you think you can find out where Chance came from? His past?" My stomach fluttered at the thought. I was excited and anxious at the same time. What if we stumbled on something I didn't want to know? What if the Jacksons were thieves? Maybe they stole Chance from some little girl who's been crying every night since he disappeared. Maybe they grabbed him from a stall at a rodeo.

I pictured Billy pecking away at a keyboard, creating fake registration papers to ensure he'd get his money from me. Although, I had to admit, Billy being savvy with a computer was a far-fetched idea. That gave me some comfort.

"I'm a member of the Quarter Horse Association," Taylor said, making a few more swipes at the Ipad with her finger before she continued. "That gives me access to online records. It allows me to look up information on any registered quarter horse."

"Really?" I asked, zoning in on the kind of information we were about to find on Chance...on my Chance. "What kind of stuff? What kind of information do you have access to?"

"Bloodlines, show records, past owners. Stuff like that." Taylor seemed to find what she was looking for on her Ipad. "Where are Chance's papers?" I stood up and unzipped a pocket on the side of my duffel bag, pulling out a thick sheet of tan paper, folded once. Taylor continued her instructions. "There should be a registration number in the upper right hand corner of the paper. Read it to me."

I read off the numbers, one by one, waiting as Taylor typed them into the online records system. I held my breath when she pressed enter and almost told her to stop. Chance was mine, as far as I knew, and I didn't want anything to change that. Would Taylor keep my secret if we found out he didn't actually belong to me?

I swallowed hard and tried to ignore the questions growing in my head, but they only multiplied as I watched Taylor's reaction to the new information. She turned her body towards me, slowly, her lips parted, ready to spew out Chance's story.

I shook my head. "I take it back. I don't want to know. Don't tell me whatever you just read." Taylor was being nice to me now, but she wasn't *that* nice. If Chance wasn't mine, she wouldn't keep that to herself. "I really don't want to know."

"Oh, I think you're going to want to know this," she said, her eyes wide as she ignored my babbling. "Chance's registered name is Fool's Gold, right?"

I nodded hesitantly.

"Do you know what Cash's registered name is?"

"Linda's horse?"

This time Taylor nodded.

I didn't know what Cash's registered name was. The only time I had spent around Cash was during the Cowboy Race and at the awards ceremony. The only thing I knew about him was that he was a gorgeous buckskin and Linda had won about a thousand championships on him. Well, maybe a thousand was exaggerating a bit.

"No," I responded. "Why does that matter?"

"Because Cash's registered name is Gold Rush." Taylor sat still, her mouth gaped open, obviously waiting for me to put the pieces together.

"Does that mean their related?"

"Yes," she exclaimed and snorted out a breath - like she didn't believe it herself. "They have the same sire, Blazing Gold. And, they came from the same barn in Texas. It looks like Chance was born at South-Cross Stables and sold about four years later." Taylor set the Ipad on her crossed legs and looked at me like I'd just won the lottery. "The trainer at South-Cross Stables is a five-time world champion barrel racer. And, Blazing Gold is her prized stallion. He's sired more champions than I can count."

The pieces of Chance's past were falling together and starting to make sense. "If Chance was sold at four, that means he probably had at least a year of training at that barn." I was amazed at this revelation, but at the same time, those things didn't really matter to me. I loved Chance before I knew his bloodlines, his training, which barn he came from. "So...does your Ipad say Chance is mine?"

Taylor cocked her head and I thought she was going to tell me I was a few bricks short of a load. "Yes, crazy." She handed me her Ipad. "After South-Star Stables and about five other names, you are listed as Chance's current owner." Taylor pointed to the middle of the screen. "See. It says Lucy Rose right there."

I let out a sigh of pure relief and let myself relax into the couch.

Taylor sat back too, thumping her slender body against the cushion and taking a minute to think. "Do you know how much Linda paid for Cash?" She started laughing before answering her own question. "She wrote a check for $20,000 when he was a yearling. Twenty thousand dollars!"

I couldn't help but to gasp.

"She paid thousands of dollars for Cash and you found a horse roaming around in the mountains with the same bloodlines and *more* training." Taylor's body shook with laughter. "Now that's funny stuff. I can't wait to tell Linda that one."

"I'm thinking she's not going to find it quite as funny." Actually, I was certain she wasn't going to find it quite as funny.

But, it kind of was.

A giggle grew and bubbled up from my chest

and soon Taylor and I were laughing together...that surprised me more than Chance's bloodlines. But, it felt good. The two of us laughed until we both melted into the soft leather of the cushions and were out of breath.

Taylor sighed, holding her stomach as she glanced at the digital clock on the microwave. "Oh, crap. It's already 6:00?"

I watched her jump from the couch. "Do you have somewhere to be?" I was being sarcastic, but Taylor opened a closet door and started scanning through the tank tops and jeans she had hanging in a neat row. I guess she did have somewhere to be.

She pulled out a turquoise tank top and looked at me over her shoulder. "You want to go to a bonfire, Lucy?"

The bonfire Taylor invited me to wasn't noted on the show schedule, but she informed me it was only a short walk away. After a quick change of clothes, Taylor and I left the trailer, walked along the white fence of the rodeo arena, and hiked through a field towards a thick patch of trees. Once in the brush, Taylor located a weathered fence and hopped over a broken board. She turned back as I hesitated, skeptical of where she was leading me.

"Come on," she said, waving her hand at me. "I promise I'm not leading you blindly into the wilderness."

I gave her a doubtful stare. "I'm not sure I trust you this much yet." Which was true.

She shrugged her shoulders, but grinned at the same time. "I wouldn't trust me either. But if you don't come, you're going to miss out on some killer barbeque. Tanner Wilkenson's Mom is like the Martha Stewart of the grill. Plus, there'll be s'mores."

I stood still for another second and then gave in. Who could resist s'mores? "I'll trust you this one time," I noted before grabbing hold of the fence and jumping over. But, as my feet touched the ground, a whiff of spiced brown sugar goodness hit my nose. Taylor and I inhaled together, closing our eyes to relish in the sweet, smoky aroma. "Okay, I believe you," I said, as my eyes opened.

"Told you so."

Taylor didn't waste any time and stepped towards a beat-down dirt path. It looked like this area of the woods had seen some traffic. "So this Tanner is a friend of yours?" I asked, following along as my stomach growled.

"Yeah, Tanner's whole family shows horses. They're at all the big events. Everyone knows the Wilkensons," Taylor said, making a sharp turn at the end of the dirt path. She pushed aside a few leafy branches and we stepped out onto a well-manicured lawn. "And, since they basically live next door to the show grounds, they have a barbeque every year on the last night of the show."

"Well, that's awfully nice of them."

Taylor shrugged. "I think they just like to party. But, whatever. They always have amazing food."

Taylor and I strolled across a sprawling lawn towards a classic red barn with white trim and an iron weather vane. We passed three square pastures, each with a few grazing horses. The fourth pasture, closest to the barn, had a wide open gate and smoke rising from a well-built bonfire. A group of laughing teens hung within range of the flames, sticks in hands.

Taylor nodded her head towards the bonfire as we passed. "The s'mores area is over there and the barbecue's next to the barn."

My mouth started watering in anticipation.

Outside the barn, there was a smoldering charcoal grill and a table full of typical summer dishes. Taylor handed me a paper plate which I filled full of potato salad, corn on the cob, baked beans, and sauced ribs. By the time we made it to one of the picnic tables, I had already finished a rib, balancing my plate in one hand.

"Hey, Taylor." Friendly faces at the table

greeted us as we sat.

Taylor smiled and flipped her blonde braid over her shoulder. "This is Lucy," she said before making herself comfy on the wooden bench.

The group greeted me in unison, as well. I recognized most of them from the show, even without their fancy outfits. And, with Taylor's introduction, they accepted me instantly. No questions asked. The group chatted away as we filled our bellies, telling stories of their horses and the show year. I listened, chiming in with one word agreements between mouthfuls. It was nice to relax and be part of the group, instead of the worker-bee for a change.

Taylor and I scraped our plates clean at the same time and I glanced at the bonfire.

"You got room for a s'more?" I asked.

Taylor licked her lips and rose from the bench. "I always have room for dessert."

"It was nice to meet everyone," I said with a wave as we left the group.

After more introductions at the bonfire, Taylor and I roasted marshmallows and created four of the best looking s'mores I had ever seen - golden goo oozing over melted chocolate and graham crackers. I sighed at the sight of them. They were almost too pretty to eat.

Taylor grabbed one in each hand. "Come on,"

she said. "I've got to show you one of the Wilkenson's colts. He was born late in the season so he's only a few days old. He's adorable."

Without question, I grabbed my two s'mores and scurried off with Taylor to the barn. We headed down the aisle and straight to an extra large stall in the middle of the barn. I held one of Taylor's s'mores as she pulled open the door to reveal a dark bay mare munching on a mouthful of hay. Next to her side was a miniature version of mom with wobbly legs and a fuzzy, black mohawk for a mane. I couldn't help it – I squealed.

Taylor looked at me knowingly. "Isn't he just the cutest thing ever?"

I wanted to reach out and touch his baby soft coat, his tiny muzzle, the fuzzy puff of his forelock. But I held back, not knowing how the mare would react. "Do you think she will mind if we get closer?"

"Tanner said she's starting to get used to people around her baby, but she's a first-time mom. She's a little nervous." Taylor took a few quiet steps into the stall. "We probably shouldn't get too close, but we can watch them from a distance."

Taylor lowered herself into a cross-legged position in the cedar bedding. I tiptoed in her steps and sat down beside her. We were just a few feet from the cracked door, giving the mom and baby plenty of room, but the mare turned her head to blow soft breaths against her colt's neck - checking to make sure he was okay with the new visitors. The bay colt responded by nuzzling his mother's cheek. With his nose pressed against her, the colt's lips wrinkled up, exposing his pink toothless gums.

Taylor's eyes lit up and she smiled at me without words, but I knew we were thinking the same thing. What a special moment we were witnessing. And, in that moment I recognized that Taylor and I shared the same love for horses, even though we lived in different worlds. Sitting there on the stall floor, just a few inches from each other, I wondered if we could actually be friends.

"Thanks for bringing me here," I whispered.

Taylor opened her mouth to respond, but a slew of footsteps and laughter cut her off. The mare's head jerked up at the noise.

"We should probably leave them alone before we stress them out," Taylor noted, pulling her feet underneath herself to stand, but stopping as she heard her name leave the mouth of a boy in the barn aisle.

"So you and Taylor Johnson are back together, huh?" The boy teased. "Or were you guys just sucking-face for the heck of it today?" He was obviously teasing Jace. I glanced at Taylor, wondering if she was offended by the boy's rude comment, but she only rolled her eyes and awaited

Jace's answer.

"Yes, Scott. We're back together. Why? You keeping notes on who I'm dating?" Another boy snickered at Jace's remark. "Or you just jealous?"

I could tell egos were flaring up and I didn't like where this conversation was going - especially since the boys didn't know we were within earshot. I squirmed, eager to make our presence known, but Taylor placed her finger in front of her smiling mouth, shushing me. For some reason, she wanted to hear what they had to say about her.

"Well, obviously I'm jealous," Scott replied and then chuckled. "Except you guys aren't going to be together long once she finds out what you did."

Now I had a view of the group through the cracked stall door. The guys stopped, facing each other, and I watched as Jace shot a dirty look at Scott.

"It's not like I meant for that to happen," Jace replied.

"What? What happened?" The third kid chimed in.

Scott continued, loving whatever he had hanging over Jace's head. "Jace didn't tell you?" He laughed at the secret he was holding.

Jace laced his thumbs in his jean pockets and shook his head. "You're such a loud-mouth, Scott."

Scott playfully punched Jace in the shoulder.

"Oh, come on. It's funny!"

The third kid was dying to get clued in. "What are you guys talking about?" he pleaded.

Scott raised his eyebrows and tipped his cowboy hat towards the third boy. "You remember yesterday when Taylor was ahead of Jace in the point totals? When she was on her way to winning the all-around championship title?" The other kid nodded his head. "You remember when she cartwheeled off her horse and took a nose-dive into the dirt?" Scott waited for the kid to nod again before continuing. "That wasn't a coincidence."

Both boys looked at Jace, slowly.

"What?" he said, shrugging his shoulders at the accusation. "I didn't mean for her to fall off. I just loosened the cinch so she'd have to stop in the middle of the class and forfeit. I didn't expect her to keep riding with a loose saddle."

The s'more I was holding rolled off my fingers and dropped to the ground as my hand popped up to cover my mouth. I whipped my head around to face Taylor. She was in the same crouched position, but the color had completely drained from her face, along with her smile. I didn't know what to do. I didn't know what to say. I could barely comprehend what I just heard. Jace, who was apparently Taylor's boyfriend, had sabotaged her ride. Worse than that, he intentionally put Taylor in danger. There were a thousand things that could have happened to her...things much worse than just hitting the dirt.

I pulled my hand away from my mouth as I remembered the minutes before Taylor's class. "Jace held Star for me while I got her bridle out of the tack room," I whispered in disbelief. "He must have loosed the girth when I wasn't watching."

Taylor looked sick to her stomach, her breaths increasing. I didn't know if she was going to cry or throw-up. Trying to comfort her, I reached over and placed a hand on her knee, but my touch only jolted her body into action.

Taylor snapped her mouth shut and leap-frogged over me, bursting through the stall door. The overly-cocky group of boys suddenly looked like they were witnessing a ghost march across the aisle. I barely had time to get to my feet before Taylor got to Jace.

She didn't let him speak. In one swift movement, Taylor circled her arm around and smacked Jace in the face - with a handful of s'more. He flinched at the attack, his hands flying up in surrender and his back hitting the wall behind him, but Taylor didn't back down. She stepped closer, glaring up at his six-foot frame with vengeance as she slowly ground the graham cracker-marshmallow-chocolate mess into his face.

"I can't believe I wasted a second of my time on you," she snarled, leaning closer and wiping the gooey leftovers across the front of his starched, clean shirt. "Don't ever talk to me again. I mean it. Don't *ever* talk to me again."

The other boys stepped back. Jace didn't utter a word.

And finishing her attack, Taylor picked her foot up and stopped her wooden boot heel down on Jace's toe, hard. Really hard.

I stood in the doorway of the stall, stunned, as Taylor turned on her heels and marched off. She stomped across the floor in a heated exit, leaving Jace cussing and hopping on one foot, but I caught her bottom lip quivering as she passed me.

I took off after her.

Taylor

Sweat rolled down my back, dampening the gauzy fabric of my shirt, and my calves burned, protesting my run through the woods. I never looked back, but I knew Lucy was following me. She called out my name at first. When I didn't reply, I only heard her footsteps.

The heat rose from my chest and into my face as I thought of Jace. *Why would he do that to me? How could he do that to me?* That good-for-nothing, lying, scum-of-the-freaking-earth...a growl rolled up my throat and turned into a screech as it left my mouth. Two girls exiting the barn jumped and scattered out of my path as I blew by. I didn't care what they thought. They hadn't just had had their hearts ripped out of their chest. They hadn't been slapped in the face by someone they thought they loved.

I wanted to get to my trailer, to be hidden away from the world while I crumbled, but the pressure in my eyes wouldn't stop. I couldn't keep the tears from coming. Instead, I made a hard left into the tack stall, whipping aside the fabric curtain as hot tears ran over my cheeks.

I dropped myself down on a stack of dirty sheets just as Lucy walked in. She took a few steps towards me.

"Leave me alone," I said, followed by a sob I was trying to hold in. "I need to be by myself." I couldn't handle being with anyone right now. I couldn't trust anyone.

With my head in my hands, I could see Lucy's boots through my fingers. They didn't move.

"I'm not leaving you alone, Taylor," she said, barely above a whisper. "You shouldn't be alone right now." Another sob escaped my throat, but Lucy didn't go away.

Jace's betrayal cut me like a knife. I thought he cared about me. I thought he loved me. Everything I thought was wrong. He sabotaged me because he wanted to win. I hit the dirt because of my boyfriend...my ex-boyfriend. The tears flew down my cheeks and I buried my face into my knees, wrapping my arms around my legs. "I feel so stupid," I mumbled into my jeans.

Lucy's footsteps fell across the ground and the sheets crinkled as she took a seat next to me. "That guy's a jerk. A complete jerk." Her words were steady, but I caught the disgust in her voice. "Nobody with any sense in their head would put another person in danger, for any reason." Lucy put her hand on my arm and gave it a soft squeeze. "He doesn't deserve you."

I tried hard to control my breathing as my jeans soaked up the tears. I stayed in that position, cradled and afraid to move until the crying slowed. My heart physically hurt, my eyes burned, and through it all Lucy never moved an inch, her hand still on my arm. She didn't tell me I was stupid for falling for Jace. She didn't remind me that I had blamed *her* for my accident. She just sat there and listened to me cry.

I raised my head slowly, setting my cheek against my knees and swallowing the lump in my throat. I bit my lip to stifle a sob.

Lucy looked straight into my blurry eyes, her lips pressed together in a straight line. "That guy deserves a lot more than a s'more to the face."

FOURTEEN

Lucy

HALF AN HOUR later, I helped Taylor to her feet, leaving the crumpled pile of horse sheets on the floor. I grabbed three bridles from the metal rack, handing one to Taylor, and we exited the tack room. We had a plan. Well, sort of.

"First, we need to find Tiera," I noted. Taylor gave me a sideways glance with her red eyes, but she didn't protest. "Just trust me."

Taylor nodded.

I pulled my phone from my jeans and dialed Tiera, giving her a shortened version of the recent fiasco with Jace. Just seconds after ending the call, a blur of pink came running down the barn aisle headed straight for Taylor. Taylor winced as Tiera wrapped her arms around her and squeezed, pressing her head against Taylor's chest. Tiera held tight, her cell phone still in her hand.

Taylor raised an eyebrow at me, stuck in the awkward embrace. I cracked a grin.

"I can't believe he did that to you," Tiera exclaimed as she pulled back, still holding Taylor's arms. "What a...what a..."

I chimed in, stopping Tiera from trying to find a word suitable for Jace. "I can't believe it either. And, he certainly doesn't deserve to win the championship title."

Taylor wiggled out of Tiera's embrace, taking a step back and a deep breath.

"Of course he doesn't," Tiera said, her mouth open in disgust. "We need to report him to the show office, to the judges. They'll disqualify him for cheating."

Taylor's voice cracked as she finally spoke. "And what am I supposed to tell the judges?" She crossed her arms over her chest, cradling herself. "That I was hiding in a horse stall at a barbeque and I overheard Jace bragging to his friends that he loosened Star's girth before my ride?"

Tiera looked back and forth between Taylor and me and shrugged her shoulders. "I think they'll believe you. I mean, why would you lie about something like that?"

"We have no real proof," I said. "It would be his word against ours and I don't think he's going to fess up. Owning up to cheating, to putting Taylor in danger, would be suicide for Jace. They'd strip him of his winnings. Heck, the association probably wouldn't let him show again. Ever."

Taylor dug her nails into the flesh of her arms as she processed my words. "Lucy's right," she said, and shook her head. "Jace will never fess up to that. He'd never jeopardize winning the title or being banished from the show ring. We're going to have to beat him at his own game."

Tiera leaned in closer, waiting to hear our plan. I filled in the details we had so far. "Taylor and Jace both have two classes to compete in tomorrow – mountain trail and the freestyle horsemanship class. Taylor feels confident she can beat Jace in the trail class, but she needs our help to beat him in the freestyle class."

Taylor jumped in. "Jace always wins the freestyle class. Hammer's spins and sliding stops are killer. And, on top of that, he just had a new ride choreographed and the music was put together by some top-notch DJ his Dad knows in LA."

Tiera's face scrunched up in confusion and I felt an explanation was in order. "I didn't know what a freestyle horsemanship class was, either, until ten minutes ago. Basically, a rider has four minutes to put on a show, set to music, and certain movements are required during that time."

Taylor continued the explanation. "The riders have to complete a lead change, stop, pivot, and present all three gaits during those four minutes. And, you can show off any other trick or talent you want to. The judges score the riders on each maneuver, but a third of your score actually comes from the audience. The louder they scream, the more points you get." Tiera's eyes widened as Taylor described the class. "But Jace knows my music. He knows my whole plan for the freestyle class because I bounced ideas off him when we were dating...the first time we were dating. For all I know, he could have stolen all my ideas to use himself."

"I wouldn't put it past him," I said. "Cheating obviously doesn't bother him one bit."

"What can I do to help?" Tiera asked, genuinely concerned.

I stepped towards Tiera and handed her a bridle. "We need to put our heads together and come up with a brand new presentation with brand new music. And, we have one day to do it."

"I'm in!" Tiera squealed making both Taylor and me jump. "It's like we're the Saddle Club or something!" She clasped her hands together and jumped on her tippy toes.

After the shock of her squeal wore off, I

couldn't help but laugh. Taylor, on the other hand, was looking at Tiera like we just teamed up with a crazy person.

"What?" Tiera stopped jumping, still holding her hands to her chest. "Was that a little too much?"

The sun cast a peach shadow over the open field and, in the last rays of light, we gathered our horses in a powwow, their noses nearly touching. From our saddles, Taylor, Tiera and I absorbed the music flowing out of Tiera's phone one last time.

The last few beats of the melody pumped through the air before Tiera lowered her phone to her thigh. "Who knew the remix music from dance class would come in handy after the recital? I'm glad I saved it on my phone."

Taylor was biting her lip, her eyes closed as she went through the routine in her head.

I rested my hand on the saddle horn. "I think we've got it down."

Taylor opened her eyes. "Maybe we should do it one more time? Just to be sure."

"Taylor, it's going to be dark soon and we don't want to wear the horses out. They've all got to be ready for tomorrow – especially Star."

Taylor paused and then nodded. "Yeah, you're

right. Let's head back to the barn." She rolled her fingers through Star's flaxen mane, smoothing it against her neck. "I just want the performance to be perfect, you know? I don't want to give Jace any advantage."

Her usually confident brown eyes revealed a hint of uncertainty and I realized Taylor was looking for my reassurance. "Taylor, you just do what you do best – ride. Tiera and I will take care of the rest."

I hoped my words sounded stronger than they felt.

After a not-so-restful night of sleep, Tiera and I sat in the bleachers, literally on the edge of our seats, watching the mountain trail class. The course, spread out across the indoor arena, was made of an array of obstacles and completely different from the classes Taylor had been competing in up to this point.

"These obstacles look freaking scary," Tiera whispered to me out the corner of her mouth.

I agreed. There were multiple log obstacles and jumps, a bridge that teeter-tottered when stepped on, and even a man-made pond surrounded by stuffed animals (not the soft, fuzzy ones). I knew Chance would take one look at that fake elk's pointy rack and he'd run in the opposite direction. Every obstacle was a test of the rider's relationship with their horse.

"Here comes Taylor," I said and we straightened up in our seats. Taylor rode into the arena at a lope and approached the first obstacle - the double log jump. "This one is right up her alley." And she proved me right as Star easily popped over both logs, looking relaxed.

So far, none of the riders - including Jace – had completed a perfect round. There were even a few riders that had to get off their horses and lead them out of the arena, without completing the course. But most had finished, making it through the obstacles in one form or another. And there were a handful of riders who rode it well, making few mistakes. Currently, Jace was in the lead with the most points and quickest time, but even Hammer had baulked at a few of the obstacles.

Loping away from the log jump, Taylor slowed Star to a walk, getting ready to tackle the miniature mountain. This obstacle was a dirt hill covered in thick branches and rocks. Taylor took her time, allowing Star to lower her nose and check out her footing. Being cautious, Star took slow steps over the closely placed objects and climbed to the top of the mound where there was a flat spot, just big enough to turn around. A 180-degree pivot was required and Star made it look easy, turning in a tight half-circle and carefully retreating down the same path.

Tiera grabbed my forearm. "She's doing awesome." There was a squeaky tone to her voice.

"Don't jinx her," I replied. "She's got half the course left."

Tiera squeezed my arm tighter. "You're right. You're right."

Next was the pond, surrounded by stuffed elk, deer, and turkeys. They approached the water at a trot until Star was just a few feet away from the edge...and she suddenly spooked. Star dug her hooves into the ground and back peddled, snorting at the herd of unknown animals. I clenched my jaw and sucked air through my teeth, but Taylor looked unfazed, allowing Star to stand still and sniff the air.

"It's taxidermy," I explained to Tiera. "Those are real hides from dead animals."

"That's gross." Tiera wrinkled her nose.

"I'm sure Star is freaked out by the smells. Her instincts are telling her to get out of there."

Taylor patted Star and seemed to be talking to her, coaxing her. Slowly, Star's neck lowered and she stepped towards the pond, all her senses on high alert. She put one hoof in the water and then burst through the shallow pond with a high-stepping trot, spraying droplets through the air and leaving the dead animals behind.

Next, the pair cantered back and forth in an S-shape through a line of closely placed trees. She swooshed through the obstacle like a gamer running poles. I looked at the clock blinking on the wall above the arena. Taylor was making up lost time, but it was going to be close. All of the top riders completed the course in around three and a half minutes. And, the clock just passed the three minute mark.

"Come on, Taylor. Come on. You got this," I mumbled under my breath, squeezing my knees with both hands. I heard Tiera muttering the same words.

Star stopped just short of the next obstacle, the bridge, and Taylor asked her to step on. This time Star didn't hesitate, getting her front feet on the wood...but she didn't expect the bridge to move under her hooves. Tiera and I gasped as Star launched her body away from the perceived danger.

"Poor Star wasn't expecting a teeter-totter!" Tiera exclaimed as Taylor rode Star into a circle, trying to calm her down. Star made her displeasure known, wringing her neck from side to side.

By this point, my fingers were digging into the metal of my seat, wrapped tightly around the edge. "I don't know if she's going to step foot on that bridge again. And, they have to make it across or they're disqualified."

The crowd was now in a murmur, watching

Taylor and the clock.

Approaching the bridge again, Star hesitated, but trusted Taylor enough to follow her cues. She moved forward, placing one hoof on the bridge to test it. The wood creaked, falling under her weight. Star waited for it to settle before following with her other front hoof. With tentative steps, Star inched her way across the bridge and then launched off the opposite end as it teetered down. It wasn't pretty, but they made it across.

"They have one more obstacle!" Tiera squealed, as we both jumped to our feet, watching Taylor and Star blaze around the end of the arena and turn back towards the gate. Taylor's blonde hair hung in the wind behind her as they soared over the last jump, a thick fallen tree, and broke into a gallop towards the finish line.

Tiera and I screamed, pumping our fists in the air as the clock ticked away. As Star blew past the electric timer, the blinking numbers stopped at three minutes, thirty-four seconds. I gasped, and Tiera looked to me for an explanation.

"It's not the fastest time, but Taylor could still win, depending on what the judges awarded her for points on each obstacle." And there was one more ride to go before the final scores were announced. That was too long to sit still. "Let's go find Taylor."

Tiera and I burst out of the arena and found

Taylor dismounted and standing next to Star. She shook her head as we got closer.

"I should have given Star more time to look at the obstacles," she said, still shaking her head. "Dang it."

She was beating herself up for honest mistakes. "You had one of the top times, Taylor. You could still easily win."

Taylor chewed her lip. "I'm going to walk Star around while the last rider goes. This wait is going to kill me." And with that, Taylor turned away and Star followed. Tiera and I were left standing by the arena.

"I'm going to walk with her," Tiera said, but I put a hand on her arm as she stepped forward.

"I think Star is the only thing that can calm her nerves right now. Let's let her be."

Tiera nodded, understanding, and we waited to hear the results.

Most of the riders, including Jace, were on their horses, gathered around the arena gate as they watched the last competitor. I scanned Jace up and down, wondering when he got the idea to loosen Star's girth or why that thought would even cross his mind.

Jace caught my stare and I whispered to Tiera. "Hammer doesn't deserve a cheating, big-headed jerk for an owner." Jace couldn't hear my words, but my face must have conveyed their meaning. He quickly broke eye contact and looked away.

Tiera snapped her fingers. "True dat, sister."

Finally, the announcer's voice cracked over the speakers, breaking my gaze. "All right, folks. We have the official results for the mountain trail class. The top three rides were separated by only a few points. As your name is called, please enter the arena for your ribbon." All chit-chat stopped. "In third place...we have Taylor Johnson."

I cupped my hand to my mouth. "Oh, crap." I scanned the crowd and found Taylor, back in the saddle and riding towards the arena. Before she could get there, the second and first place winners were announced.

Jace's name was last.

"Oh no," Tiera whined. "What does that mean? Does Taylor still have a chance at the championship?"

Taylor jogged Star through the center of the group gathered at the gate. Her shoulders were back, her equitation in perfect form, but when she passed Jace, the look on her face could have peeled paint from barn wood. Jace flinched. A wave of fear flashed across his face. Did he think Taylor was going to rat him out? She probably should've.

But Taylor didn't slow down. She didn't speak one word. She rode into the arena and picked up her yellow ribbon, even flashing a smile for the clapping audience.

And I scraped together the words to answer Tiera's question. "That yellow ribbon means Taylor needs to get a blue one tonight. No other color will win her the championship."

FIFTEEN

Lucy

TAYLOR WEAVED THE last of the silky ribbon into Star's braided mane as I walked out of the tack room, fastening the buckle of my borrowed black chaps.

"I told you they'd fit you. You look good in chaps." Taylor shot me a smile as she tied off the last braid. "At least I'm not making you wear a leotard." She winked and I chuckled at the thought.

"You would've gotten a fight out of me if you tried to stuff me into one of those things. Spandex? Ugh." I grinned back, looking over Taylor's getup. She sported the same leather chaps, but instead of a black t-shirt, her outfit was topped with one of Tiera's dance leotards. Metallic purple and blue fringe hung from the back of her sleeves and draped her shoulders. Her long blonde ponytail fell down her back in curls. "But, the leotard suits you."

She cocked an eyebrow. "Thanks...I think."

"Okay, you guys. I'm ready," Tiera announced as she jogged down the hall in a matching black leotard with fringe, black tights and a metallic purple tutu. She hopped along in her cowboy boots, carrying her ballet shoes in her hand. She was all smiles. "Horses and dance. The perfect combo!"

Chance wasn't as sure about her statement, snorting at her bouncing tutu as she jogged past.

"Looks like the horses are ready, too," Tiera said, patting Georgie as he tried to get a mouthful of fringe.

Star, Chance & Georgie stood patiently, tacked up and full of braids and ribbons. Their gleaming coats were sprinkled in glitter. I took a deep breath, wiping my sweaty palms on my shirt. "Okay, girls. Let's do this."

Dusk settled over the outdoor arena as we rode up, side-by-side as a team. The wooden bleachers were packed, the overhead lights blaring, and the announcer's voice boomed through the evening air. It was just as I pictured it when Chance and I ran barrels the other day. Only this time it was for real. I swallowed a growing lump in my throat and glanced at the other girls. All three of us were quiet, lost in our own thoughts.

Taylor was serious but relaxed, swaying with Star's stride. And her straight face warmed when she caught me looking her way. I knew how much this meant to her. I now knew how hard she worked for each one of her wins, how much she cared about her relationship with Star. I wanted Taylor to win this championship, not in spite of Jace, but because she had earned it.

We slowed to a halt, joining the group of riders waiting by the closed gate and I jumped as an electric guitar squealed out of the speakers, followed by crashing drums. It sounded like a rock band was exploding somewhere in the arena.

"Jace is riding," Taylor said, peering through the crowd.

Both Tiera and I craned our necks, trying to get a glimpse, but I only caught a flash of bay as Hammer whizzed by and the rock song played on. Whatever Jace was doing, he was doing it at high speed. The audience hooted and whistled, rising to their feet at the end.

"That was Jace Brooks, folks. Current leader for this year's Northwest Stock Show All-Around Championship title. He is certainly giving his fellow competitors a run for their money, isn't he?" The announcer's words shattered through the cheers as Jace trotted out of the arena on Hammer, pumping his fist in the air.

"And next we have another top contender for the title, Taylor Johnson. Her performance tonight is called *The Dance-off.*" At his introduction, the riders in front of us parted and I felt my lungs constrict. This was it.

Taylor, Tiera and I rode in a line, together, stopping in the brief safety of the chute - only a few feet from stepping into the arena. All three horses pricked their ears towards the bright lights. Star stood in the middle of the pack, Georgie and Chance edging her in.

In the few seconds of quiet, Taylor dropped her reins, resting them on Star's neck and reached her hands out for ours. I grabbed hold, giving her a hand a squeeze, and I watched Tiera do the same from the other side.

"Thank you," Taylor mouthed, first to me, and then to Tiera. Her two simple words brought peace back to my mind as the lights went dark.

Taylor

My hands were still warm as I picked up the reins

and watched Lucy and Tiera leave my side. They directed their horses towards the single spotlight on the black arena floor. Light glistened off the metallic ribbons floating from Chance and Georgie's hair and butterflies moved through my belly as I watched them trot, knowing I would join them soon.

The audience was hushed now, but I planned on making them roar. Nothing about performing made me nervous - only excited. *This is what I live for.* And it was time to show everyone what I could do.

A second spotlight moved in my direction and I brushed Star with my legs. She obliged and we stepped out onto the dirt, inching towards the horses as Tiera dismounted.

Lucy took Georgie's reins from Tiera, guiding both geldings out of sight and leaving Tiera in the middle of the arena. In the circle of light, Tiera stood perfectly still, her legs together and toes pointed out. Her arms were suspended in front of her, bent at the elbows and her fingers nearly touched. Her slick blonde bun glowed in the light. She was the silent image of a ballerina.

Star and I approached and stopped to face her. In the quiet of the arena, Tiera completed a curtsy, crossing her legs while bending forward, holding the outer edges of her tutu.

I cued Star to respond and she began lowering her chest, shifting her rear into the air. She folded one front leg underneath herself, taking her knee to the ground while the opposite leg stayed straight, extended in front of her. Star's nose nearly grazed the ground as she held the bowing position and the crowd whispered.

I winked at Tiera as the soft classical music started and both Star and the ballerina rose to stand. I shifted in the saddle, realigning myself before the real riding began.

As the violins played over the speakers, Tiera arched her arms in the air and began spinning, one leg floating through the air in a circle around her. Her body rotated in the ray of light over and over until she stopped abruptly, facing me with two legs on the ground again.

Star's ears pricked when she knew it was our turn. I lightly guided the reins to the right, pressing my left calf to her side, and Star began crisscrossing her front legs. I centered my body in the saddle, balancing myself as she picked up speed. She moved her front around her rear in an increasingly intense spin...faster and faster. Her flaxen mane, laced with ribbons, blew parallel to the ground and the audience became a black, soundless blur until Star stopped on a dime, facing Tiera again.

There was a deafening pause before the whistles, hoots, and hollers brought a grin to my face. I was warming up the crowd.

Tiera didn't wait for the audience to quiet before she began floating across the arena, arms in the air and her legs following as she leaped in an elegant zigzag. Her tutu bounced and her toes touched with each jump - like a graceful gazelle. At the end, she turned back towards me with a beckoning curtsy.

I put my fingers to the brim of my black cowboy hat and tipped my head, accepting her challenge as Star pushed forward into a canter. We looped around Tiera a few times, stretching into a quick pace before turning across the diagonal of the arena.

Taking a breath, I eased Star into a slower speed and prepared us for our first lead change. With a subtle move of my leg and a hint of a weight change in the saddle, Star bounced from her left lead to her right lead with ease and we received a gracious clap from the crowd. We executed a second lead change just as we passed Tiera and she dramatically set her hands on her hips, getting a giggle from the audience.

As we rounded the end of the arena, I gathered my reins in my fingers and began cantering straight down the long middle of the arena.

"Here we go, girl," I said, sucking in a breath. "This is what we have been practicing for." Star gathered herself and we began a line of single lead changes. With every stride, Star changed her lead, practically floating through the air. She bent her body from left to right to left to right, each stride zigzagging with the change of direction. We danced together, merely skipping down the center of the arena - moving as one unit with the rhythm of the music.

As we finished our last lead change, my focus zoned back to reality and I immediately noticed the screams from the stands. Reacting to the noise, Star rung her tail, knowing she did a great job, before coming to an abrupt stop in front of a pouting ballerina. I tipped my hat once more, this time with a wink.

At the wink, Tiera flew off into a stream of jumps. Launching herself through the air, her legs rose until they were parallel to the dirt, over and over again. Finishing her last jump, she landed just a few feet from Georgie and hopped up into the saddle. Feet in the stirrups, Tiera joined Lucy as they trotted their horses to the middle of the arena.

The crowd hushed again, waiting for my response, as Lucy pulled a long, purple ribbon from her saddle bag. With one swift throw, she tossed an end to Tiera. Tiera grabbed the ribbon and they both backed their horses until Georgie and Chance were a few horse lengths apart, still facing each other and pulling the ribbon tight.

The music morphed into a fast tempo, increasing the crowd's anticipation. But, I wasn't done yet. I wasn't going to leave anyone sitting in their seats.

Reaching forward, nearly laying on Star's neck, I threaded my fingers under her leather bridle, gently pulling it over her ears. I waited for Star to release the bit from her mouth before letting the whole thing drop. The bridle piled into a heap at Star's hooves and the arena gasped as one.

Still stretched across Star's neck, I took a second to close my eyes and inhale her sweet scent. Kissing Star on her glossy coat, I whispered, "Let's finish this, baby girl. Let's show them what we can do."

Sitting up in the saddle, I took in the vision of the mob surrounding me - all leaning on the edge of their seats - and my heart pumped faster, following the speed of the music. Without a bridle, I was completely reliant on my relationship with Star. But, I didn't have a doubt in my mind. Star and I were a team. We worked as one unit and I could always count on her.

With a slight movement of my leg, we pushed off into a canter, circling the arena and increasing our speed with every lap. Raising my arms up, the fringe whipped from the back of my sleeves and I pumped my arms in the air, asking the crowd for more. They responded with whistles and hollers which swelled as we moved into a gallop.

As we turned towards the middle of the arena, I

asked Star to decrease her speed, just enough that we were balanced for our final act. Slowing, I locked my eyes on Lucy and Tiera - sitting in their saddles and holding a single ribbon which closed the gap between their horses.

Star moved underneath me like an extension of my own body. I felt every movement - each leg as it hit the ground, each breath as it blew from her lungs.

And, a stride before the ribbon, Star gathered her whole body and catapulted us into the air. Her ears slapped back against her neck as she put all she had into that jump.

Leaning forward, her mane whipped me in the face as we soared upwards. And, as Star's body evened out over the top of the ribbon, I sat up and launched my own arms into the air. My sight was blinded by the blaring spotlight, but I knew the vision we were creating. We were flying through the sky – bridleless and seemingly weightless. The light was bouncing off Star's chestnut coat as the ribbons and fringe lashed in the wind.

We rolled through the air in slow motion, but when gravity connected us with the ground, the crowd's roars filled every crevice of the arena and my heart burst with pride. I immediately latched onto Star's neck as we cantered off. Happy tears fell from my eyes. I couldn't put into words how much I loved Star. But I knew she understood.

The crowd's cheers continued, but my performance didn't feel complete. I looked back at the two girls that built me up when I was down and I wanted to be next to them. I wanted to share this moment with Lucy and Tiera.

Star and I glided across the arena and stopped between Chance and Georgie. Grabbing the girls' hands again, we raised our palms to the dark sky, smiles plastered on our faces and a silent bond passing between our eyes.

Who knew I'd come out of this show with two new friends.

SIXTEEN

Taylor

THE BRIGHT MORNING sun warmed my arms as I reached up to hand Star a carrot. Popping her head out of the open trailer window, she snatched it up, breaking the veggie in two with one crunch. As she chewed, Star pinned her ears and snaked her head at Chance - who was watching patiently from the next trailer window. He batted his dark lashes at me.

"Be nice, Star," I said, patting her on the nose. "Would you like a treat too, Chance?" His chocolate eyes enlarged as I stepped towards him and, when I offered the second half of the carrot, Chance wrapped his lips around the gift and gently removed it from my hand. "Did you see that, Star? You might want to take a tip or two on manners from this guy."

I chuckled and Star replied with a hasty snort before two swift honks grabbed my attention. I turned to find Tim driving the big rig alongside my trailer. The diesel truck rumbled as it approached and both Tim and Linda were waving their hands out the open windows.

"Call me when you get back to the ranch so that I know you made it safely," Linda instructed.

"Will do," I said with a smile and a wave.

"Great job this weekend, Ms. Northwest Champion! Keep up the good work with Star and we'll be headed to the World Show next year." Linda flashed one of her rare beaming smiles and I knew she was proud of me. Her words warmed my heart. "Tim and I will see you in a few months. Enjoy the rest of your summer at Red Rock, Taylor."

"Take care, Princess," Tim chimed in with a wink before rolling the rig towards the driveway. I smiled as they departed, knowing I would miss them, but having a renewed excitement to enjoy the rest of my summer at the ranch.

Ready to head out, I turned my attention back to the horses, but caught a glimpse of red as I spun. As the six-horse trailer passed, a cherry red mustang emerged, following in its path. The car crawled unusually close to the bumper, trying to hide in the trailer's dust, but I stood watch, holding my gaze as the mustang approached.

Beneath the dark windshield I saw Jace's outline, his cowboy hat pulled low over his eyes. I was certain he couldn't wait to get out of here. He raised two fingers off the steering wheel in some kind of greeting – or maybe his version of an apology - and I simply gave him a nod. I didn't rat Jace out to the authorities, but I think like he learned his lesson – cheaters don't win...in the show ring or in life. *And,* if you cross Taylor Johnson, she will smash a s'more in your face and beat your pants off in the arena.

"Good riddance," I muttered under my breath at the back of the mustang. "I don't know what I saw in you in the first place." And I wasn't going to waste another second of my time or energy on Jace. I had better things to focus on.

Turning back to the trailer, I closed each window, prepping for the drive back to the ranch. Just as I snapped Chance's window shut, I heard a car door slam. Feet pounded across the pavement and I was tackled in a bear hug before I could even turn around.

"I caught Lucy in the barn and gave her a big hug, too. I'm going to miss you guys so much," Tiera squealed, hugging mc tighter.

"We'll miss you too, Tiera," I said, turning to hug her back. My words even surprised me. "Let's plan on a trail ride in early September when I get back to Linda's barn, okay?"

"Okay. You and Lucy better call me with updates from the ranch," Tiera instructed as she gave me one more squeeze. "I might just have to join you guys there next summer."

Tiera released her embrace and jogged back to the waiting Mercedes. I called after her. "Maybe we could both learn how to rope a steer?"

"That would be awesome!" Tiera shouted as she hopped in the car and waved goodbye.

I completed one more safety check on the hitch and then climbed into the driver's seat just as Lucy opened the passenger door. She jumped in holding a disposable plastic cup in each hand and balancing her cell phone between her shoulder and her ear.

"This one's for you," she said, stretching her arm out to me. "Mocha with extra whip cream."

I took the drink from her hand, excited to get it to my lips. "Yum...thank you," I replied before taking a sip.

"I was talking to Taylor," Lucy commented into the phone as she snapped her seatbelt into place. "Yes, it's just Taylor and me driving her trailer back to the ranch. And, no, I promise we won't kill each other on the way back." She caught my eye and stifled a giggle. I grinned, realizing how much our relationship had changed in just a few short days.

"Is that Casey?" I mouthed to her and she

nodded, wrapping up her conversation.

"Yeah, I'll fill you in when we get to the ranch. I've got a lot to tell you. Talk to you soon." And, with a smile, Lucy set her phone on the truck's leather seat, next to the gigantic trophy – which was strapped in with its own seatbelt. Her fingers left the phone and touched the etching on the trophy's plaque, reading the words aloud. *Taylor Johnson, Lucy Rose & Tiera Alexander ~ Northwest Stock Horse Champions*. I still can't believe you had the show staff put our names on the trophy too."

I took another sip of my mocha before turning the key to start the truck. The engine roared to life. "It's our trophy, Lucy. It was a team effort."

ABOUT THE AUTHOR

Brittney Joy

Cowboy Boots or Muck Boots always have been Joy's shoe of choice. An animal lover to the core, her parents didn't know what they were signing up for when they put her in a summer horse camp at the age of ten. She was hooked.

Horses quickly became her true passion in life. At twelve she started working at a local stable— cleaning stalls and leading trail rides. At thirteen her parents finally broke down and bought her first horse, Austie. Austie was a spunky bay Quarter Horse/Saddlebred cross with a perfect white heart on her forehead. Joy grew up on Austie's back and learned so much from that spirited mare. When it came time to go to college, she packed Austie along too.

Joy and her family now live in their own little piece of heaven in the Oregon countryside. They stay busy taking care of their two horses, one chicken, two naughty goats, and one very adorable dog. When Joy isn't writing, she's riding or reading. She wishes she could do all three at the same time.

For more information on Brittney Joy, Red Rock Ranch, and upcoming equine-adventures, please visit:

http://brittneyjoybooks.sqsp.com/

Sign-up for Joy's newsletter and be informed of new book releases, fun contests, book promos & discounts, bookish secrets, writing secrets, book recommendations, and pictures of her horses & pup:

https://brittneyjoybooks.squarespace.com/newsletter

Happy Trails!
~Brittney Joy

AUTHOR'S NOTE
Brittney Joy

Thank you for joining me in telling the story of Red Rock Ranch. I hope Lucy, Taylor, Tiera, and all their furry friends touched your heart the way they touched mine.

If you loved the book and have a minute to spare, I would really appreciate a review on Amazon, GoodReads, or the site where you bought the book. It's okay if it's short! A star-rating and a sentence or two make a big difference. Your review is greatly appreciated as it will help new readers find my stories. Your reviews also inspire & motivate me to continue to write more stories in this series.

Also, I love, love, love hearing from readers so don't be shy about reaching out via email or social media!

Thank you and Happy Trails until we meet again!
Brittney

Website: **http://brittneyjoybooks.sqsp.com/**

Books by Brittney Joy

Lucy's Chance (Red Rock Ranch, book 1)
Showdown (Red Rock Ranch, book 2)
Rodeo Daze (Red Rock Ranch, book 3)

Deck The Stalls (Horse Stories for the Holidays,
Short Stories Anthology - Contributor)

OverRuled (The OverRuled Series, book 1)
OverRun (The OverRuled Series, book 2)

*(The OverRuled Series is young adult fantasy
series & includes a main character who has a
magical connection to horses)*

RODEO DAZE
The Red Rock Ranch Series, book 3

Lucy always dreamed of competing in a horse show— but she'd never thought it'd become reality.

When a big competition comes to Three Rivers, the whole town's talking about who will win the title. Lucy is happy to stay on the sidelines to watch— until a tragedy causes her to step up and participate with her horse, Chance.

With frenemy Taylor as her coach and a bitter new rival to challenge, Lucy isn't sure she can handle the pressure. Plus her relationship with Casey is growing, and she needs to know where she stands. Lucy doesn't want to be "just friends" with the cute cowboy.

Can Lucy get over her stage fright and make all her dreams come true— in the arena and with Casey?

Printed in Great Britain
by Amazon